I thought ⟨...⟩ reading
books. Th ⟨...⟩ ntic bag of
mistake ⟨...⟩ happens in
the books. So this is my book ⟨...⟩ school
isn't like the books I read. But boarding school *is* like
this book, of course, unless you've decided without even
knowing me that I'm going to be a big liar, but there's
nothing I can do about that.

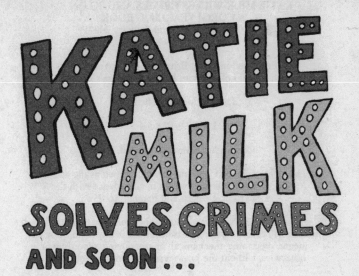

KATIE
MILK
SOLVES CRIMES
AND SO ON ...

ANNIE CAULFIELD

KATIE MILK SOLVES CRIMES AND SO ON ...
A CORGI YEARLING BOOK
978 0 440 86686 2 (from January 2007)
0 440 86686 3

Published in Great Britain by Corgi Yearling,
an imprint of Random House Children's Books

This edition published 2006

1 3 5 7 9 10 8 6 4 2

Papers used by Random House Children's Books are natural,
recyclable products made from wood grown in sustainable forests.
The manufacturing processes conform to the environmental
regulations of the country of origin.

Set in 12/16pt Janson by
Falcon Oast Graphic Art Ltd.

Corgi Yearling Books are published by
Random House Children's Books,
61–63 Uxbridge Road, London W5 5SA,
a division of The Random House Group Ltd,
in Australia by Random House Australia (Pty) Ltd,
20 Alfred Street, Milsons Point, Sydney, NSW 2061, Australia,
in New Zealand by Random House New Zealand Ltd,
18 Poland Road, Glenfield, Auckland 10, New Zealand,
and in South Africa by Random House (Pty) Ltd
Isle of Houghton, Corner Boundary Road & Carse O'Gowrie,
Houghton 2198, South Africa.

THE RANDOM HOUSE GROUP Limited Reg. No. 954009
www.kidsatrandomhouse.co.uk

A CIP catalogue record for this book is available from the British Library.

Printed and bound in Great Britain by
Cox & Wyman Ltd, Reading, Berkshire

FOR MOLLY AND JAZZ,
ALWAYS INSPIRING

CHAPTER ONE

I thought I knew about boarding schools from reading books. This was my first mistake in a gigantic bag of mistakes. What happens is not the same as what happens in the books. So this is my book about why boarding school isn't like the books I read. But boarding school *is* like this book, of course, unless you've decided without even knowing me that I'm going to be a big liar, but there's nothing I can do about that.

For a start, in the books – those other ones, not mine – people go to boarding school, have adventures, get kidnapped, solve crimes and so on. They don't start talking about how interesting it might be to go to boarding school and have their mum say: 'What are you, nuts? Boarding schools are thousands and thousands of pounds and for the kids of Lord and Lady Fru Fru, not nurses, so have a biscuit, Katie, and go to bed.'

And she didn't even mean the biscuit because she'd forgotten to buy any.

So I didn't think about boarding school any more. None

of my friends were going to such schools when we finished at the Heights Primary, north London. We'd all go to the same secondary school in north London, just a few miles from The Heights, and carry on being quite happy and, as the teachers liked to say about me, 'average'. And I had plenty to do as far as solving crimes was concerned without having to go to some fancy school.

In my own way I had been solving crimes from a very early age. My grandad would tell me about crimes and ask me who I thought had done them. He'd tell me all the clues and give me hints to help me be a top detective like him.

Grandad looked after me when Mum was at work because he was all there was to choose from. My dad was 'gone off' since I was a baby, far away and disappeared.

The only other person in our family was Auntie Apricot. She was a very weird person and we hardly ever saw her. But then, suddenly, when I thought everything was always going to be average for ever, she completely changed my life.

Really, Auntie Apricot was my mum's auntie, Grandad's sister. She lived in a massive flat full of furry carpets and glass things with gold edges. She had *Apricot* embroidered on everything – her towels, her pillows and on a big cushion on her enormous leather sofa. Which was a bit strange, considering her name was really Maureen. Maureen Milne. But when she'd got rich, she'd changed her name to Apricot Milne because she felt this was more classy. And she went berserk if people, like Grandad, ever forgot and accidentally called her plain old Maureen.

She'd got very rich from being a cleaner. Just her at first, then some other women, until eventually, all over London, office blocks were cleaned by women who worked for my Auntie Apricot and wore apricot nylon overalls she'd designed herself. They also wore specially made apricot-coloured rubber gloves and apricot nylon hats that made them look like mad walking fruit.

By the time of the special overalls, gloves and hats, Auntie Apricot didn't clean any more herself. She sat in her office, smoking, organizing everybody else and answering the phone in a put-on posh voice saying: 'Apricot Milne Services, may we rescue you from dust, dirt and chaos?'

She drove my mum up the wall. That's why we didn't see her much. She was always criticizing everything and telling Mum to find a new husband. Grandad said he was scared of her. He said he couldn't really explain why, except he felt it was sensible to be scared of someone who'd changed their name to *Apricot*.

Then, just at the start of the summer, when she should have been going on her usual luxury holidays, Auntie Apricot died of heart failure.

Despite saying she was scary, Grandad was sad when she died.

At the funeral I saw him walk away to stand by himself.

I followed him and gave him a tissue in case he was going to cry.

'I'm not one for crying, Katie, love, you know that,' he told me. 'But there used to be five brothers and sisters in my family and I'm the last one. Suddenly I feel very lonely.'

I told him he still had me and Mum. He smiled and said I was absolutely right.

But later, when I was telling Mum how I'd been sure he was going to cry, she said he had always been lonely since her mum, my grandma, had died, years before I was born. Mum said she thought Grandad was still so sad about Grandma that he'd lost interest in everything except television and us. And Mum didn't see what could happen to change him and make him start a whole new life.

By the way, you might be thinking: how come if Grandad was a top detective he wasn't interested in that? But solving crimes was just a game he played with me. Really he was a security guard in a chemist's and all the crimes for the game were from things he'd seen in films, telly programmes and detective books. He was only racing around catching murderers and thieves of the crown jewels in his head – in real life he had to stop people stealing toothpaste.

I thought that was how life was for us: OK, not starving or anything, but only ever exciting inside our own heads. Until Mum had a letter about Auntie Apricot's money. The letter said there was a big arrangement to do with me and the money, involving a lot of lawyers and things that made my mum say, 'Blimey!'

So we had to get dressed up, go to a lawyers' fancy office on the other side of London and listen to a long reading out of Auntie Apricot's will.

In the will, she said that as my mum hadn't got a proper husband, I could run wild if I didn't go to a good school with nuns. A boarding school. And there would be loads of money for me afterwards when I was eighteen. But if I didn't go to a school with nuns, the particular one Auntie Apricot mentioned in her will, then I would get nothing, and all the money would go to Auntie Apricot's local church, to spend on anything they pleased.

Just as I was thinking what an amazing thing to happen – I was getting to go to boarding school and I'd have amazing adventures and – it all started going wrong. My mum had jumped to her feet and was shouting at the lawyer men: 'Was she nuts? Making me send my Katie away to some place with nuns? Not for all the money in the world, never!'

And the lawyer men were staring at her like she was nuts because if you weren't used to her my mum could sound very insane when she was shouting.

'Hang on a minute, love…' Grandad was saying to her.

'No,' she said. 'We're out of here. Come on, Katie.' And she grabbed my arm to make me move.

I couldn't move.

All the papers that said I could go to boarding school

and have an interesting time were there on the desk. The lawyers said it was a top place, full of princesses and children of millionaires – but my mum was shouting crazily and saying I couldn't go?

No way was I moving.

CHAPTER TWO

When they'd stopped being scared and staring, the lawyers handed my mum some brochures for the boarding school Auntie Apricot had picked out. So she could think the matter over.

'Nothing to think about,' my mum said. But she took the brochures because I was looking at her trying to make a face like I was going to cry. Which I might. And she knew that face.

All the way home she drove like a maniac and went on about how Auntie Apricot was only being spiteful, how she knew Mum didn't hold with nuns and a whole lot of church and this was sheer spite . . .

We did go to church — Mass, as it was called in our Catholic religion — once every few months. My mum had always said she wanted me to know about it but not feel 'oppressed' by it.

'Oppressed' was some kind of feeling of being bored and depressed and generally squashed by life that my mum said she didn't want for me. Being 'oppressed' was something you could get from nuns apparently. My mum had been at school with nuns who she said not only oppressed her, but tried to fill her head with weird and frightening ideas...Unfortunately in the car she wasn't telling me what the weird and frightening ideas had been – they sounded as if they might have been interesting. She just kept going on about the 'total out of the questioness' of boarding schools with nuns and not letting me get a word in edgewise.

I showed Grandad the brochures for the school – Mum didn't want to look. The school was a big old building in the countryside. There were pictures of girls in uniforms getting prizes and looking happy eating picnics. There were boring pictures of computer rooms and classrooms in modern blocks behind some pretty gardens. There were pictures of cosy little bedrooms and it said the school was a happy family. There were a couple of pictures of nuns, smiling and looking like they must be the ancient great-great-grandmothers in this family.

We had old nuns at our church; they sat at the back, played hymns on guitars and sang like cats in a bag. There were also nuns in books I'd been given by Auntie Apricot. Nuns and saints who seemed to look very beautiful and saved people who were starving. Then there were nuns I'd seen in films at Christmas who saved people being chased by Hitler or criminals. In my view, nuns got up to interesting stuff and didn't care if anyone thought they were silly or looked peculiar.

When we were looking at the brochures Mum finally started banging around in the kitchen making tea. This silent banging in the kitchen was the worst phase when she was angry. It meant she was storing up ideas for her final, absolute-death-to-anything-you-might-think final argument.

I said quietly to Grandad, 'Isn't she even going to listen to me? I really want to go.'

He looked at me thoughtfully. 'It's not the school she minds, Katie. It's you going away. Being at school miles away, not even home for the weekends. That's what I'd mind too. We'd miss you.'

I'd been so excited I hadn't thought of anything like that.

'But, Grandad, in the brochure it says we can go home for weekends after three weeks, or you can visit.'

He nodded sadly and said, 'We're used to seeing you every day, that's all.'

My mum came out with plates and cutlery. She picked the brochure up off the table and I thought she was going to throw it across the room. Instead she just stared at it.

'The thing is,' Grandad started to say, 'all that money Katie could have when she's eighteen, imagine how useful—'

'No,' my mum interrupted. 'She is not going to that terrible place just to be rich years and years from now.'

'I don't think it can be that terrible,' Grandad said. 'My sister was strange but she meant the best for Katie.'

Mum made a grunting noise and went to stir something

in the kitchen. I followed her and said, 'Mum, I will miss seeing you every day, but can't I just try it?'

She turned round with a wooden spoon dripping soup in her hand. I waited for shouting but she stared at the spoon for ages, as if it was doing the talking to her.

'Tell you what,' she said to the spoon, 'we'll take a look at the school and then decide.'

I jumped at her to hug her – she dropped the spoon in fright and said: 'That isn't saying yes, it isn't saying yes!'

But she knew me, and knew it would do for yes.

CHAPTER THREE

Once we'd looked at the school, met some nuns and convinced Mum it wouldn't be terrible or the total ruin and destruction of me, there was another problem. Lists and lists came of things we had to buy.

'For crying out loud, it's like equipping an army!' my mum shouted at the lists, because she was a bit of an exaggerator to say the least.

And Auntie Apricot hadn't given Mum any money towards these extra things: uniforms, books, sports equipment... When I saw the huge prices I felt guilty and said maybe it was a bad idea. I told Mum I wouldn't exactly die without going to boarding school. But all she did was laugh and say: 'Pay me back when you're eighteen.'

I also needed to take sheets, towels, nighties, a dressing gown, slippers and suitcases to put them in. Mum insisted all these had to be new. Even though she had to get them out of the catalogue and would be paying for the rest of the year, she wasn't having me going to a posh school with old nighties and slippers. That's what she was like, shouty and going on about things, but if she saw I really wanted something with all my heart, she'd have exploded the sky to get it for me.

The school had been a hotel once, so girls slept just two in a small room with a wash basin in the corner, which was very homely.

When I arrived for my first day, the other girl in my room wasn't there yet. Mum made up my bed and helped me unpack my blue and white uniform, so new it felt crunchy.

'I hope this girl will be nice,' she said as she laid my new towels on the chair and put my new fluffy slippers at the end of the bed.

A red-faced nun came in, Sister Ita. She said it was time for Mum to say goodbye.

I'd already said goodbye to Grandad back in London. He'd kept making silly jokes so he wouldn't seem sad about it.

Mum did look sad and hugged me so tight I couldn't breathe. She made a sort of sniffy sound like she was trying not to cry, but I ignored that. I was eleven now and years of experience had taught me that paying attention just encourages mothers to really start howling, with wet tissues and blurred-up lipstick everywhere, which is hideous and embarrassing for all concerned.

I thought I should probably look sad too, so she didn't feel I didn't care about her, but I was kind of in a hurry to get on with things. Get on with having the adventures I'd read about in the boarding-school books – spies, mysteries, kidnappings, crimes and general assorted adventures.

I waved as Mum drove off in her old brown car. She carefully manoeuvred it round shiny Mercedes and Daimlers belonging to other girls' parents, then she was gone.

The fact that my mum was poor and driving something that looked more like a rusty oil drum than a car was not a bad thing – in the books about boarding schools, the girl who is the most popular, good at everything, solves the crimes, catches spies and so on, is usually from a poor family. The rich type of girls at boarding schools just sit around being rich – they don't have to do anything special or interesting. Although quite often they turn out to be spies, or get kidnapped, so watch out for that.

Anyway, there I was. On my own, hundreds of miles from my house. An older girl in her blue and white uniform was telling me to go back to my bedroom, put on my uniform and wait until I heard a bell for tea. That's when I got to my room and met the girl who smelled of wee. Sorry to say wee so early in the story but Bernadette Kelly did smell of it, a lot.

You might not mind someone who smelled of wee. You might decide the girl who smelled of wee was funny and kind and ought to be your best friend, regardless of her smell problem. But you would be very unlikely to decide this if the wee-smelling girl was Bernadette Kelly.

I was looking in the wardrobe mirror, trying to

remember how my grandad had showed me to tie the blue and white tie.

'Can't you tie your tie?' Bernadette Kelly said when she came in. 'New girls never know how to tie their ties. I suppose you're Katherine Milne – I have to share a room with you. I'm Bernadette. Everyone calls me Bernie.'

'Everyone calls me Katie,' I said.

'No one calls you anything yet,' she snapped. 'You're new.'

This was when I noticed she smelled of wee. She was ginger haired with a skinny, pointy face, and the smell came right across the room at me. And she was looking at me as if it was me stinking the place out.

If she'd been nice I might have told her that everyone at my old school actually called me Katie Milk, because I was as pale as pale, even in the hottest, longest summer. So with Milne sounding very remotely like milk and me having very dark brown hair, almost black, which made me look more pale and milkish in contrast...I could have told Bernadette all this about my name but obviously being new was some kind of ridiculous thing that didn't allow you to say things about your name. I couldn't think of anything else to say, so I got on with tying my tie. Luckily I remembered how to do it so she couldn't comment any more about that.

Bernadette sat on her faded pink duvet and looked at my chair. 'You can't have those towels on the chair. You have to put your towels on the shelf in the top of the wardrobe and hang your dressing gown on the back of the door.'

I wasn't going to move my towels and dressing gown straight away just like that. At the school I'd gone to before, if you gave in to people right away the next thing you knew they'd be nicking your trainers and your dinner money.

I looked at her and said, 'Your dressing gown is on your bed.' It was a horrible dressing gown, I noticed, frayed and faded. But I had a feeling she deserved it.

'So? I'll move it in a minute,' she said. 'I'm just telling you where things are supposed to be so you won't get in trouble when Sister Ita comes round later. She's very fussy about us keeping our rooms tidy. But if you want to get in trouble with the nuns straight away that's up to you.'

She flung herself in her chair and sat there, glaring at me. I carried on looking in the mirror for a while, just so she wouldn't think I was easy to push around. But I was going to move my towels in a minute. It probably wouldn't be a good idea to be getting in trouble straight away.

I looked weird in the uniform – old-fashioned, like someone from a world-war film.

'What are you looking at?' Bernadette asked, scowling at me.

'The uniform. I've never been to a school with a uniform and nuns before,' I said as I went to move my towels.

'You're lucky then,' Bernadette Kelly said. 'All the nuns here are horrible. They act nice when your parents come to look round the school but then they change. You'll see, they change completely. You'll hate them.'

The nuns had seemed nice when I'd come up with my mum and Grandad. We'd met Sister Patricia – old, small and made a squeaky noise before she spoke, as if she had a switch in her throat that needed oiling. Her nun's veil seemed to be too big for her, so it was crooked, slipping around her head. She would be my class teacher and I'd liked it when she'd said, after a squeak, 'We just have a lot of fun in this school, a lot of fun.'

We'd also met the head of the school, Sister Maria. She was young, tall and beautiful. Like a film star dressed up as a nun. She spoke very quietly, like low music.

'Of course there's plenty of fun,' she'd said. 'But our girls work hard and go on to do great things in the world. Great things.'

Then she talked about girls who'd been there who were famous journalists and doctors – and a nun who was very famous for saving poor people with diseases. I'd liked the sound of that too.

These kinds of things didn't interest my mum. She wanted to know if girls got upset, being miles from home for weeks on end.

'Oh yes,' Sister Maria said, with a smile that showed completely perfect teeth. 'We are very aware that can be a difficulty. For the first term we always put a new girl to share a bedroom with a girl who has been here a while, so they don't feel confused about things.'

'That's a nice arrangement,' my mum had said.

It had seemed to me it was a nice arrangement too. But

I hadn't thought I'd be put with someone like Bernadette Kelly. Instead of helping me not be confused about things, she just kept talking about how horrible everything was.

According to Bernadette, the nuns were horrible, the food was vomit-making, the weekends were boring because there were long walks in the countryside and the country-side was ugly...

'It'll seem weird being at school at the weekend,' I said, just to interrupt her complaining.

'Where did you go to school before then?' she asked me.

'London.'

'Yes, you sound like you come from London.' Bernadette made a face like not only did I smell, but the whole of London smelled.

'You don't sound like you come from London,' I said, because that's all I could think of. Actually she sounded very posh. But not in a nice way like an actress or some-thing. More like she had some beads stuck up her nose.

'My parents live in Hong Kong,' she said. 'They're very rich. My father runs a bank. I go to Hong Kong every holiday. Or sometimes my mother comes here, just to see me. We go to a hotel and have a thoroughly luxurious time. We thoroughly enjoy ourselves. I've told my mother I hate it here so I expect I'll leave soon.'

Then Bernadette told me she'd been at the boarding school since she was seven. So it didn't seem to me that her mother was listening to her too thoroughly.

'When will you leave?' I asked her, to test her.

Bernadette looked furious. 'My mother says that she arranges her entire life to suit me and my brothers, so if she says she'll do something she will. And she bought me a bicycle this holidays, not for a birthday or anything, just as a present.'

A bicycle sounded quite good. I'd had a kid's bike but I'd grown out of it now. Still, I didn't really like the sound of Bernadette's mother. I didn't quite believe that she would do things if she said she'd do them.

'But if you've been here since you were seven and you're eleven now...' I said, to show I wasn't sure of these stories about her mum.

'Listen!' Bernadette said crossly. 'I'm not some dumped kid like Chiquita Morris – I have excellent parents and soon I'll live with them all the time. So don't you dare ever call me a liar or I'll kill you!'

I did think she was a liar. Certainly about killing me. How would she do that? With her smell maybe but . . . What was this about a dumped kid? That sounded interesting. 'Who's Chiquita Morris?' I asked.

'She's disgusting.' Bernadette came towards me, pointy nose sticking out. 'So disgusting she has to have a room on her own. She's been here since she was four. She has no father and no mother and just has to live here all the time.'

This sounded tragic, not disgusting. 'No father and no mother? That's pretty bad,' I said.

'Oh, don't feel sorry for her, that's a big mistake.' Bernadette screwed her face up into a sharp cat's bottom type of look. 'Chiquita always tells lies and we think she steals things. Also, she's so fat she's disgusting. And she's so dim, she's in our class even though she's nearly thirteen. You'll hate her, everyone does.'

I wondered who or what there was in the world that Bernadette Kelly didn't hate?

I didn't want to talk to her any more – she was ruining my idea of how boarding school was supposed to be. But there was no escape from her. The bell rang for tea and Bernadette bossily informed me I had to follow her outside.

'They give us a picnic on the first evening: stale sandwiches and soggy biscuits in the garden. Come on, you have to go everywhere with me for the first term, sit next to me in class and listen to all my advice.'

'What if your advice is wrong?' I asked her.

But she didn't hear me, she had already rushed out into the corridor shouting, 'Come on then, don't keep making me have to hurry you up, or looking after you's going to be even more of a boring nightmare than it is already.'

And I decided that her advice would definitely, always be wrong.

CHAPTER FOUR

The garden was sunny and girls queued up at a table where red-faced Sister Ita was handing them a cheese sandwich, a little packet of biscuits and a plastic cup of juice.

'That's Chiquita Morris getting her sandwich now,' Bernadette hissed as we took our place in the queue. 'Don't look at her.'

But, of course, I did.

Chiquita Morris didn't look anything like the girl Bernadette had made me imagine. For a start, she wasn't that fat. Maybe she seemed fat to someone all spiky like Bernadette but she didn't look much fatter than me and people always said I was 'average build'. As I've explained, 'average' was a word people seemed to use about me a lot, not always in a nice way, but we're not talking about me now, we're talking about Chiquita Morris, who is of immense importance in this story.

To me the most noticeable thing was Chiquita's hair: very long, black, wavy hair – almost to her waist. She had light brown skin, huge brown eyes and eyelashes that curled up like a doll's. Actually, Chiquita Morris was beautiful.

Other girls were chatting and laughing in the queue but not Chiquita; she just stared ahead of her at nothing in particular. She moved slowly, as if her arms and legs were too heavy for her. She sat down with her food on a garden bench all by herself.

'Doesn't she have any friends?' I asked Bernadette, because I had no one else to ask.

'No. She doesn't deserve any and I already told you – don't feel sorry for her. She gets loads of pocket money because she's got her own bank accounts. She's really spoilt so she doesn't care and just lives here all the time as the huge pet of the nuns.'

She didn't sound spoilt to me.

'But wouldn't she prefer friends to nuns?'

'No one can be her friend.'

'How come?'

'Because people have been her friends and felt sorry for her and invited her home for the holidays and she turns out to be a big thief.'

Bernadette was so annoyed I guessed she was the one who'd been Chiquita's friend and invited her home, but I was wrong.

'No, of course it wasn't me who invited her. Just listen, will you, or I won't tell you the story,' she said. 'It was Danielle Kirkham-Byles who Chiquita went to stay with and she stole some of Mrs Kirkham-Byles's jewellery. So no one invites her any more and she deserves horrible holidays with just nuns.'

I still felt sorry for Chiquita. And where there was a girl who stole, there were going to be crimes. At least I was going to have crimes to solve.

'Anyway,' Bernadette said as we got our food, 'stop asking stupid questions. I have to talk to my friend now.'

Her friend was another small girl with ginger hair and freckles, but she wasn't as spiky looking as Bernadette.

'Hi, Fiona, this is my new girl, Katherine,' Bernadette said to her friend, pointing at me.

Straight away after saying hello, Fiona told me her parents lived in Belgium and her father was an important international politician.

Then Fiona pointed to the girl beside her. 'This my new girl, Sarah, her father's a major in the army.'

Sarah looked as though she'd been crying.

I didn't like the way Bernadette and Fiona were talking about us new girls as if we were some pets they'd just bought. I expected Bernadette was going to complain about her pet soon, when she found out I didn't have a proper father, let alone one with some fancy job. But no, Bernadette had a complaint I wasn't expecting.

'Katherine's from London,' she said, 'and she's a bit of a show-off.'

Fiona looked at me as if I was covered in slime. I was about to say that I didn't think I was a show-off, compared to people who went on about being incredibly rich or having important international fathers, but Fiona asked Bernadette in what ways was I a show-off?

'Oh, you know, just acts like she knows everything,' Bernadette said.

'No, I don't,' I said, and got a bit ratty because, I'm sure you'll understand, I'd just about had enough of false accusations and wrong names. 'And, by the way, no one calls me Katherine, it's Katie, just Katie.'

'Listen,' Bernadette said. 'You just got here. You don't know how to behave to be popular. You don't know anything.'

'So?' I said. 'So what?' Not clever, but it was something to say and something needed saying.

'Bernadette's the best fighter in this class,' Fiona said. 'I bet you don't know that.'

I didn't know that, but Bernadette was so small and spindly she must bite people to win.

'I can fight. I can fight anyone,' I said. I wasn't sure I could but it was worth a try.

'Liar,' Fiona said, and pushed me.

I didn't see how it had all gone wrong so fast but now I was going to have to push Fiona back and probably fight Bernadette, probably get bitten by her.

My grandad had said to my mum, 'The thing is, the sort of girls she'll be with at that school will be nice. There'll be none of the trouble there is at schools around here. None of those rough boys we get around here.'

Poor Grandad. For one thing, he didn't know that girls

are worse than boys any day of the week for fighting. They only stop fighting when they get a bit older because they get into make-up and boys and want the boys to think they're feminine. But any time there are no boys looking, girls fight.

Bernadette said, 'We can't fight her, Fiona, she's my new girl – I'll get in trouble.'

'I'm not scared of fighting you,' I said to Bernadette, because you had to say that kind of thing in situations like these, even if you didn't want to fight in a million years.

'See what I mean?' Bernadette said. 'She's really big-headed.'

Suddenly Fiona grabbed my arm and gave me a Chinese burn. I kicked her shin hard to get loose. Sarah started crying and Bernadette shouted at me, 'Look what you did, stupid!'

I decided they were all pretty stupid and started to walk away from them. I couldn't believe I'd had to kick someone on the first day. I couldn't believe I was being called a show-off and blamed for crying other new girls... So much for quickly becoming popular and leading everyone against kidnappers, spies and criminals.

It was almost as bad as the first day at The Heights school when the girls from the Burnt Oak Estate got me just for looking at them funny. Or so they said.

Almost as bad. The Burnt Oak Estate girls would have laughed their heads off at a Chinese burn. One of them had a knife when she was nine, but she got taken away to some kind of special school.

Most people on the Burnt Oak Estate had houses with broken windows and broken fridges in their gardens. Rubbish from the high street blew around their streets and no one ever cleaned up. Grandad said the kids who lived there would be lucky not to all end up in special kinds of schools because the government didn't care if they had rubbish on their streets or enough food or anything. I don't know how true that was but they were scary kids.

The gardens around the nuns' school were beautiful, full of rose beds and fountains, like a park. No rubbish or broken fridges had ever been near this place. I looked at a fountain, gushing out of a statue of a little stone lady in a stone evening dress, splashing onto some fat, sleepy goldfish in the green below. I watched the water and the goldfish, calming down, forgetting about the stupidity of fighting for no real reason with people I really didn't know. Stupidity, but seemingly a thing that happened at any kind of school.

Bernadette ran up to me. 'What are you doing?'

'Nothing,' I said. 'Watching the fish.'

'I thought you were going to tell the nuns.'

'Tell them what?'

'OK, look, if you stop being so big-headed we'll give you another chance. Come on, don't look at those fish, they're disgustingly gross. I want to play rounders against Danielle. Are you good at rounders?'

I didn't think I was. I wasn't good at any kind of sports at my last school but when I was there I'd discovered a trick to do in sports – I would fall over a lot and make people laugh. That way they didn't mind me being useless. Definitely, in my past experience, if you weren't good at something, the next best thing was to be really deliberately bad at it, so people liked you for being funny.

'Danielle Kirkham-Byles thinks she's great,' Bernadette said as I followed her. 'But she's really dim, disgustingly dim.'

On a big patch of grass in front of the main school building, girls from my year were gathering. At the centre of them was the girl Bernadette told me was disgustingly dim Danielle.

Although I was seeing so many new faces, Danielle was someone I'd particularly noticed. She seemed older than eleven, perhaps because she was so confident. She was taller than the rest of us, with a long blonde plait and a suntan. She probably lived somewhere glamorous. She sort of bounced when she walked and always seemed to be laughing. She was someone you could tell was always going to be in charge because people would want to follow her. She had a slight Scottish accent, like someone who read the news – even her accent sounded pretty. She'd had a crowd of people around her every time I'd seen her; people listening to her and wanting her to like them.

Ideally if I was going to be the person at this boarding school who caught spies, solved crimes, et cetera, I should be more like Danielle. More an obviously popular and in charge type of girl. But if she was dim, maybe she'd be dim at solving crimes and have to let me be in charge. And if she thought I was funny, perhaps she'd like helping and say: 'When it comes to crimes we have to follow Katie Milk because, although she makes us laugh, she also knows best about spies, crimes and so on.'

But for the moment Danielle did seem to be naturally in charge of everyone and everything.

'Pick a team, Bernadette,' she said. 'First I pick Indira, my new girl. You should pick yours, it's only fair, they don't know anyone.'

'OK,' Bernadette said, and you could see all over her face that she just hated Danielle.

I wished I was Indira, the elegant-looking Indian new girl beside Danielle. How much better to be learning about the school from someone who laughed and bounced than from smelling, complaining Bernadette.

'That Indira's a princess apparently,' Fiona said after she was picked by Bernadette too.

Indira looked like a princess. All delicate and fine-boned, ready to have a bath in flower petals at any moment.

'Trust Danielle to get put with a princess,' Bernadette said. 'Just something else for her to show off about.' Then she picked crying Sarah for her team. Crying Sarah had stopped now but looked like she'd start again in a second.

'Yes,' Fiona said to me. 'You think you're a show-off but Danielle's the worst in the whole school. She thinks she's really good at sports but Bernie's much better.' Then she nipped my arm. 'I haven't forgotten you kicked me but we're saying we're equal, OK?'

'Yes,' I said. 'Let's forget about it.' Although, of course, I wouldn't forget about it, ever.

As the two teams for rounders were chosen, most people shouted for Danielle to pick them and looked fed up if Bernadette picked them. I could understand that.

'Bernie always wins,' Fiona said, as if she'd read my mind. 'People are stupid to prefer Danielle – Bernie's is always the best team to be on.'

I noticed that Chiquita Morris was nowhere to be seen. You'd imagine after spending all her holidays alone with the nuns she'd want to be at least near the people in her class, but she seemed to have vanished.

Bernadette batted first but got stuck at second base. I was to go next. I have never been able to hit a ball with a bat. I just can't make my arms and eyes work right. I missed once and Bernadette shouted: 'Come on, concentrate!'

I knew that no amount of concentrating would ever help, so it was definitely time to be funny. I made a wild swing at the ball, spun round and pretended I'd gone round so fast I fell over. I heard a couple of people laugh. That was good.

'What are you doing?' Bernadette shouted.

I got to my feet, pretending to stagger around dizzy.

'Stop showing off!' Bernadette shouted.

I looked at Danielle to see how she was reacting. She was making a very sensible kind of face.

'Come on, other people are waiting for their turn,' she said, as if she thought I was pretty stupid.

The next ball came and I was out.

'You're useless,' Bernadette said as I went to sit on the grass, out of the way. The game went on with all Bernadette's team doing quite well. Even crying Sarah turned out to be a very fast runner.

'You better field over there,' Bernadette said when the teams swapped. 'I expect you can't catch much either.'

I was sent to the edge of the grass, so far away no one was likely to hit the ball near me.

As bad luck would have it, Danielle hit the ball really hard and it landed right by me.

'Throw it back, throw it back!' Bernadette screamed. I tried but it landed a very long way from her. She ran to get it and meanwhile Danielle was running, scoring rounders, being cheered by her side in a way none of our team had cheered for Bernadette, even though it did seem like Bernadette had hit just as far and could run just as fast.

'Useless!' Bernadette screamed at me.

I decided that if I was so useless she could manage without me. I walked over to a bench at the side of the grass and sat down. I hadn't come all this way from London to be told I was useless by a girl who smelled of wee.

I was confused and very depressed with myself. I seemed to have drawn attention to myself in all the wrong ways. I might as well have held a sign over my head that said: 'I'm very useless and weird, no point making friends with me.'

For the first time I thought about home. How, seeing as it was after tea, I'd be watching telly with Mum, or Grandad if she was working late. Suddenly I had a terrible feeling like I was going to cry.

'Never let people except me and your mum see you cry.' That was something I remember Grandad saying when I'd had trouble from the Burnt Oak Estate kids, and I'd stuck to it all the way through my old school.

I remembered another thing Grandad would say when I was worried or upset. He'd say, 'In any difficult situation just be yourself, Katie, and you'll win the day.'

So far I'd been pretty much myself and wasn't winning this day at all. And the day wasn't over yet.

For Grandad's sake I would squash my eyes shut so no tears came and try harder to win what was left of this strange day.

CHAPTER FIVE

A bell rang. The girls stopped playing and Bernadette shouted at me, 'Come on, we have to go to study hour now!' Then she shouted at Danielle, 'My team's winning, remember! We'll finish this game tomorrow!'

'Fine. If it's that important to you.' Danielle laughed, flicked her blonde plait and walked away. She was followed into the building by her team, all wanting to be near her. The straggly, miserable-looking people hung around with Bernadette, and I had to join them.

I realized that most of what had gone wrong was Bernadette's fault. If I'd been new girl to someone laughing and nice I could be enjoying myself – instead of being scowled at and told to hurry up, like I was a dog.

In the small classroom, Sister Maria was waiting for us. She stood behind her desk, watching us as we selected desks – or rather Bernadette selected a desk and pulled on my sleeve to go where she'd chosen.

All over the room, new girls were being pulled by the sleeve to sit with the person looking after them. I started to sit down and Bernadette pulled my sleeve again.

'Not yet,' she hissed.

I realized everyone was still standing, looking at Sister Maria in silence. At my old school everyone had rushed to sprawl in their seats, chattering and laughing until the teacher shouted: 'Be quiet! Be quiet! Shut up!' about five times.

I couldn't imagine Sister Maria shouting. She was so calm and beautiful – you'll remember I'd noticed that the first time I met her when we'd been shown around the school, but now there was a new thing to notice. She was slightly scary. She'd never need to shout. She could just look at people with her cold grey eyes and make them feel ashamed they'd even thought of doing something wrong.

Once everyone was assembled in silence, she said in her low voice, 'Good evening, Year Seven.'

And everyone chorused back, 'Good evening, Sister Maria.'

Sister Maria waited a moment, looking at us as if she didn't like us, and then she said, 'You may sit.'

Everyone sat down, still no talking, not even a whisper.

'As this is the first evening, you have no homework,' Sister Maria said, walking away from her desk. 'You will each be given a book from the shelves. You will read quietly until study time is over.'

Not only could you not imagine Sister Maria shouting, you couldn't imagine her laughing, or eating, and certainly not ever going to the toilet. She was like a cold stone angel in a holy statue. Not one of the angels who turned up at Christmas talking to old shepherds in a field about stuff going on in Bethlehem and generally being quite friendly. She was more like one of the tall shining angels who had a sword for cleaving sinners. A seriously holy angel, who had no time to bother with mere mortals and say 'be not afraid'. The type of angel who would just stare at you and cleave you or move on, depending on what they thought of your behaviour.

With long elegant hands, Sister Maria started picking books from the shelves. She told us to pass them along the desks until everyone had something to read. I hoped I'd get a good story with crimes.

'I may ask you to comment on what you've read at the end of study,' Sister Maria said, when the slow process of passing along was over and everyone had a book on their desk. I wasn't brainy but I always remembered stories I'd read so I wasn't worried about this.

Then I saw they weren't storybooks. They were books about science, or history, or serious matters. Mine looked OK, lots of pictures, all about some artist called Monet who painted flowers in a blotchy way. Bernadette Kelly had a book about the Industrial Revolution, all steam trains and drawings of machines to make cloth. I noticed that Chiquita Morris had a book called *Chemistry Is Fun*. Obviously not for Chiquita, who was staring at it as if she wanted to cry. Then she did start crying. Unashamedly crying her eyes out. Someone, maybe Bernadette, made a slight laugh.

'Chiquita Morris, what are you crying about?' Sister Maria asked, as if she was sick and tired of her.

Chiquita Morris didn't say anything, just sniffed a lot.

'Do you have a handkerchief, Chiquita?' Sister Maria looked at her, all disgusted.

Chiquita nodded, brought out her handkerchief and blew her nose noisily.

'That's better. Now just settle down, Chiquita.' I wouldn't say that Sister Maria said this kindly, but it was a little bit kinder than she had been.

'I have to go to my office to make some telephone calls,' Sister Maria said to all of us. 'No one is to leave this room. If anyone needs the lavatory they are to wait until I come back. And no one is to talk, is that clear?'

Everyone nodded. And then, as she left the room, they all stood up. Bernadette had to pull my sleeve to get me to stand up.

'Don't you know you have to stand when an adult comes in or goes out?' she said when Sister Maria had gone. 'Sit down now. Don't talk.'

She said that but she immediately started talking to Fiona, who was sitting on the other side of her. 'Looks like Chiquita's going to cry all the time this term as well.'

I don't think Chiquita could have heard, but even so it was more of the meanness of Bernadette. Meanness that seemed to have no end.

Chiquita was still sniffing and wiping her nose. All around the room people had started whispering.

Bernadette was talking about Sister Maria now. 'I bet she's making phone calls to her boyfriend.'

'I bet she doesn't stay a nun much longer,' Fiona said. 'The pretty ones always leave.'

All sorts of conversations seemed to be going on all over the room and no one seemed to notice Chiquita was still crying. I handed her my book about the painter with its blotchy pictures of flowers.

'Swap with me,' I said. 'This is much more cheerful.'

Chiquita looked at me, really shocked, as I took her *Chemistry Is Fun* book. She turned some pages, looked at the paintings and seemed to agree that at least it was more cheerful to look at. She gave me a tiny, tearful smile and continued turning the pages.

'You shouldn't pay her any attention,' Bernadette whispered. 'She just cries for attention.'

I didn't care. Whatever the reason, crying was crying. I concentrated on trying to read about why chemistry was fun. After half a page, I wasn't convinced.

Around me, little whispers were going on. I overheard fragments, mostly people talking about what they did on their holidays. I heard Danielle talking about going horse-riding with her older brothers. I'd been on a horse once at a seaside when I was about five – it didn't sound like this was the same kind of thing.

These girls didn't talk like me or live lives like me. For a start, they all talked about 'my parents'. At my old school, half the kids had families like mine, where the father was 'gone off' in some way. My friend Brian's father was in jail for something or other. Sue's dad had gone off when she was five. Only Chiquita Morris seemed to have some kind of arrangement that wasn't exactly as it should be, with one mother and one father together. In fact, Chiquita sounded as if she was an actual orphan.

In the boarding-school books, in half the stories I had ever read, it was orphans who were the heroic ones. They had terrible lives, then solved some crimes or escaped from someone's evil clutches, had a few more terrible things happen but then lived fantastically happily ever after. Of all the horse-riding, very rich and living-in-glamorous-countries girls in the class, it was probably Chiquita who would be the best friend to have if I wanted to be involved in any adventures and live to be fantastically happy.

Just as I'd realized this, the door opened and Sister Maria came in. The girls started to stand up.

'Sit down,' she said sharply.

She sat behind her desk and looked at us. We looked at her. She seemed to look each one of us right in the face, taking her time. It seemed likely she was going to yell at us at any moment but she just said quietly: 'From my office at the far end of the corridor I could hear talking in this room. I said, no talking.'

She looked at us. Everyone looked down at their desks because those grey eyes were now like a death ray.

'I am very disappointed to be confronted with this type of disobedience on the very first evening of term.' She paused, frighteningly. 'So, everyone who was talking, raise your hands and I'll put a bad-order mark in the register beside your name.'

She took a large blue book out of the desk drawer. Several people put their hands up immediately, including Bernadette. Chiquita Morris put her hand up, although I didn't remember her talking.

In my old school we never owned up to things. Certainly not small things like talking. I was amazed at these girls, automatically putting their hands up and asking for trouble. Even Chiquita, who hadn't done anything. Well, more fool them. I wasn't putting my hand up for saying a few words to someone who'd been crying.

Sister Maria was making marks in her big blue book. 'You may put your hands down.'

Then she looked steadily at us for a while longer. 'It sounded to me as though every girl in this room was talking. Are you sure that everyone who was talking has owned up?'

Everyone looked at their desks, including me. I started to feel like maybe I should own up, but surely it was too late now. Surely she'd give up and stop staring at us in a minute. It wasn't as if we'd set fire to the place. In my last school there were boys who were always setting fire to things and the police came and talked to everyone one by one until they owned up. That was fair enough, setting fire to things was a serious and insane thing to do. But we were going through all this for talking. Was Sister Maria going to call the police for talking?

Suddenly I heard a voice behind me. Danielle.

'Sister, I'm sure she's just forgotten about it but Katherine Milne was talking.'

I couldn't believe my ears. Danielle? Who'd seemed so cool? What was wrong with her? Was she sick of being the most popular girl in class? Did she want to do some kind of experiment on what it would be like to be the most unpopular snitch going?

'Stand up, Katherine.' Sister Maria looked as if she was sucking an inside-out lemon down her throat. 'Were you talking?'

'Well, yeah, one sentence because . . .' She soon scared me quiet with those eyes.

'You've let everyone sit here, uncomfortable and waiting all this time, knowing you were to blame as much as the girls who owned up. This is dishonesty and cowardice, Katherine. The talking itself isn't what matters. What disturbs me is that on your first evening here, you've shown yourself to be deceitful and cowardly. So you'll understand why I think this is serious enough to merit a telephone call to your parents to discuss a suitable severe punishment.'

A gasp went out around the room. I thought I'd better explain, in spite of Sister Maria's scary eyes trying to freeze me, that I'd a good reason to be talking.

'But I only said one sentence and it was an emergency,' I stammered.

'An emergency?' Sister Maria looked down her nose at me. 'Did the room flood? Did a lion come in the door?'

Every creepy girl in the class was laughing. Except Chiquita, who was staring at me, sorry for me, I hoped. Sister Maria tightened her lips back into her lemon-sucking face.

'No, girls, I shouldn't have said that. This isn't a frivolous matter. I'm very disappointed to find there's a new girl in this class who can't be trusted. Your punishment will be severe, Katherine, because I want you to learn what is not tolerated in this school. Now, I'm too irritated to take this class for study any longer. I will tell Sister Ita you are all to go to bed early. All of you go upstairs to your bedrooms and no talking on the stairs.'

This all seemed very temperamental for someone who looked so calm. This all seemed a lot of punishment for a scrap of talking.

We stood and shuffled out, Danielle in the lead. Of course no one dared talk outside the classroom or on the stairs, but people kept looking at me as if I had a disease. At the top, as soon as we reached the corridor with its long line of little doors to our bedrooms, a complete nightmare erupted. Danielle stopped, folded her arms and looked at me as if I'd just leaped up behind her and cut off her plait.

'Thanks a lot for getting us all in trouble,' she said, and a little group gathered around us, including Bernadette.

I didn't understand what was happening. Danielle seemed such a happy, popular person, why was she doing this? Then it occurred to me that Danielle might not have realized that this snitching problem could ruin her popularity.

I felt it was up to me to put Danielle straight about being a snitch, for her own good in life.

'How could you do that?' I said. 'How could you tell on someone over nothing, it makes you look such a creep.'

She seemed really surprised by what I'd said. She looked around at the others, who also seemed to be very surprised. Then Danielle took a step back, put her hands on her hips and looked down her nose at me.

'Well, if we're calling names, I have to say, I don't like cowards and liars. I'm disgusted by them.'

I couldn't believe how she was talking, like she was Sister Maria in a girl's skin.

She walked off with a very superior smile, all her little gang around her saying things like, 'Well done, Danielle.' The only people left with me were Bernadette Kelly and Chiquita Morris.

'Sorry,' Chiquita said to me. She had a funny voice, croaky, like someone with a very sore throat. 'It was my fault.' Then she went away, leaving me with just Bernadette, who was glaring at me as if she wanted to punch me.

'I can't believe I've got you as a new girl,' she said. 'It's bad enough here without this.'

I went into the bedroom because I could feel the wanting-to-cry feeling coming over me. Thankfully, Bernadette didn't follow me right away because I just needed a minute's peace to take it all in.

Never mind about what I'd read in boarding-school books about girls who caught spies, solved crimes and so on. How could I manage to be that kind of girl when I wasn't even managing to be just normal at this school? Not only was I not making friends, I was managing to make enemies with every second breath I took.

I thought about my friends from The Heights school, Sue and Brian and Glen. My friends who liked me and knew who I was. They were all going to still be at the same school. What had I been thinking of, wanting to come to this nightmare place instead of being with my friends, who had always thought I was funny and never called me useless, big-headed, or any of the things I'd been called in the first few hours at this new place? My friends, who had normal ideas of what was normal – like not leaping around telling tales over nothing.

I supposed we were meant to get washed and ready for bed. I looked for my wash bag where my mum had put it under the little sink in our room.

'You have to get changed before you get washed,' Bernadette said when she came in.

'I know that,' I said. 'I was just looking for my wash things.'

'And as you sleep nearest the window you have to draw the curtains.'

I slammed the cupboard under the sink shut and drew the curtains. Outside, the hills around the school were getting dark. Just a few car lights were moving. Only a couple of lights were on in the village below. It looked scary out there. Not like London, where everything was bright all night. London. Where you went to school with people who weren't maniacs.

Bernadette was sitting on her bed, looking at me.

'You've only just got here and already you've got Sister Maria calling your parents,' she said, as if I'd just stabbed everybody. 'That's so disgusting.'

'I didn't deserve it,' I said, and started to get changed.

'And,' Bernadette said, 'you let Danielle look great. How stupid is that?' Then she went off down the corridor.

I got changed into my new night things. I washed my face with my new flannel and cleaned my teeth with my new toothbrush. There wasn't anything my mum hadn't got me new for this school.

Down the corridor I could hear Sister Ita's Irish accent.

'Bernadette Kelly, go to your own room and get ready for bed immediately.'

I got into bed and pulled the duvet right over my head. I didn't want to hear anything else Bernadette had to say.

I could hear her moving around. Occasionally I could smell her. I thought if the worst came to the worst in an argument I could say something about her smelling of wee.

Sister Ita came in and said, 'Goodnight, girls. Lights out. No talking.'

The lights went out. I could hear Bernadette breathing in the darkness.

After a while she whispered, 'Are you awake?'

I didn't say anything. Sister Ita had just said no talking. How come they had this mania about not talking in this school? And how come everyone in this school was always talking when they weren't supposed to but it had turned into such a disaster for me over one sentence?

'I know you're not asleep,' Bernadette said. 'You must be really scared.'

I had to answer that. 'No, I'm not,' I said.

'You should be. No one hardly ever gets their parents phoned up. In all last year only one girl did and she ended up getting expelled.'

'For talking?'

'No. She bit a nun. I expect you'll do something like that next,' Bernadette said. 'It's not fair. I don't want a new girl like you. I hate it here enough anyway.'

I didn't speak to her again. I listened to Sister Ita saying goodnight as she turned out lights all down the corridor. Then the whole old building was silent.

Outside was silent. No traffic, nothing.

I remembered looking at the map with Grandad. The nearest town to the school was five miles away. There was just a village down the hill with a couple of shops. Nowhere to run to if you were thinking of running away and using your pocket money for a ticket back to London.

I couldn't do that on the very first night. Not when

Mum had just bought me so many new things. And where would I be going exactly? If I got out into that dark countryside, I could be lost on the hills for days before I found the town and the station. The nuns would tell the police, the police would tell Mum and Grandad – they'd think I might be dead as well as ungrateful and be so upset.

Better to stay where I was and have them phoned to say I was a liar and a coward. They knew me. They'd know it wasn't true. They'd agree with me that what I'd done wasn't anything like being a liar and a coward. They'd understand why I'd thought one sentence to poor Chiquita was an emergency. And they'd understand that telling tales was the work of creeps.

I felt braver when I thought of Mum and Grandad and how they knew who I really was. My own self, who would somehow manage to wake up tomorrow in this awful place full of creeps and win the day.

CHAPTER SIX

When I first woke up, I was extremely confused about where on earth I was. I seemed to be in a strange bed in a strange place. Then I remembered – I was in a strange bed in a strange place.

Beside me, Bernadette Kelly was asleep with her mouth open, dribbling onto her faded pink duvet cover. On the other side, light was coming through the curtains. Reaching out, I managed to pull back one curtain to see the day. The hillsides around the school looked beautiful in pink early morning light. A low mist was around the hills, like steam coming off the land. I noticed sheep over in a field to the left – sheep of all sizes hurrying somewhere. A man was putting out some kind of food for them, that's where they were off to. For the first time I saw what Grandad might mean by saying to Mum, 'It could do her good to spend some time in beautiful countryside, instead of stuck here a hundred yards from the North Circular road.'

As the disastrous events of my first evening at the school came into my thoughts, they seemed less disastrous. It was as if some elves sent by Grandad had got into my brain in the night and fixed a few things.

One of Grandad's sayings was, 'Making a mistake isn't a mistake. Not putting it right at the first opportunity is a mistake.'

So I had made a mistake. I had not exactly told a lie but I hadn't owned up to talking. I knew that if they told my mum, she'd say, 'You should have owned up.' Because owning up was the kind of thing all adults everywhere went on and on about because it made it easier for them to tell you off.

As for Danielle snitching on me the way she did, that definitely fell into the category of what my mum would call 'not minding your own business' – an extremely bad thing in Mum's thinking. But the snitching part of it had been Danielle's mistake. And possibly had been useful in showing me she wasn't as fantastic as she appeared at first glance.

My mistake, the not owning up, I could try and put right the first opportunity I had to talk to Sister Maria. I would tell her that at my old school you could get your block knocked off on the way home for owning up. I would also try harder to explain that I had been talking for a good reason. I would also beg Sister Maria not to phone my mum and upset her as she had spent a lot of money getting me new things from the catalogue and Argos.

As for the overall general disaster of everyone instantly hating me? I couldn't see a mistake to put right there. I would have to try and figure that one out once I'd made sure I wasn't on the road to being expelled.

Suddenly all this big thinking was interrupted as a bell rang: a loud electric bell that seemed to make the whole building jump.

'What's that?' I asked Bernadette, who opened her eyes wide.

'It's the bell for getting up,' she said sadly. Then she rolled onto her face and started sobbing.

'Bernadette?'

Her sobbing turned into loud, world-come-to-an-end howling. She'd been so horrible to me but someone crying so much was just something I couldn't stand, whatever they'd done to me. I jumped out of bed and knelt down beside her.

'Bernadette, Bernie, what is it? What's wrong?'

'I ha-hate it here,' she sobbed, crying so hard she could hardly get her words out. 'I didn't want to come back. I hate it here.'

'But why, Bernie?' I hadn't had a great time so far, but was it really that bad?

'I want to be with my mother and my little brothers. I don't want to be here. They say it's for my own good so I can go to hospital for my operation when I get to the top of the waiting list. But I know there's hospitals in Hong Kong, my brothers were born there. I don't want to stay here just to have an operation. Why can't I wait in Hong Kong? Why can't they hurry up? I'm sick of having something wrong with me so I always smell like I wet myself. How can I be popular if I stink? I just want to go home.'

At first I was so glad I hadn't had to use the wee smell in an argument. Then I felt ashamed that I'd gone on and on to myself in my head about her smelling. There was something serious wrong with her. Serious enough for an operation.

'Bernadette, you have to be brave and wait,' I said, putting my hand on her sweaty ginger hair. I'd seen my mum do that to sick people – it was supposed to be good.

Bernadette stopped crying, pushed my hand away and looked viciously at me. 'Get off me, you. One of the reasons I'm miserable is because of you!' She sprang out of the other side of her bed and put on her dressing gown, not looking at me again.

'Listen, Bernadette,' I said. 'I was just thinking about all that and I realize it was a mistake not to own up. In my old school people didn't own up because they'd get called a wimp or get beaten up.'

'Don't speak to me,' she said, going out of the door. 'I don't want to be friends with you.'

I stood in the middle of the bedroom, feeling really stupid for being sorry for her.

Sister Ita came in, pink-faced and not quite angry-looking, but almost. 'Everybody up? Where's Bernadette?'

'I think she's gone to the toilet,' I said.

'Lavatory,' Sister Ita said. 'Nicer to say lavatory, I think, don't you?'

I had no strong feelings on the matter so I just nodded.

Then Sister Ita surprised me by losing her crossness and nearly smiling. Although she did remain very pink.

'I'm glad to see you on your own, Katherine, because there's a little illness Bernadette has that you should understand about. Did anyone tell you about her little illness?'

'She just explained it to me.'

'Good, that's very good. Because if people don't understand these things they can be cruel to her. But hopefully she'll have an operation soon and be right as rain. Now, I hear from Sister Maria you've made quite a bad start, Katherine. Let's see how good you really are – get washed and dressed and be first to line up for breakfast on the landing like a very good girl.'

Off she went, the nearly smile disappearing and her face back in the look of someone ready to start an enormous argument.

So obviously no one could be cruel to Bernadette. But why had no one ever told Bernadette not to be cruel to people? Life, as Grandad often said, wasn't fair.

I hurried to get washed and dressed. Bernadette didn't speak when she came back in, so I left her to sniff and get dressed without any interruption from me. But when I was heading out for the landing she asked me where I was going.

'Sister Ita told me to be first in line on the landing.'

'You have to make your bed, stupid. And you should wait for me or you won't know what to do.'

'Bernadette,' I said, returning to fix my bed, 'I am not stupid.'

She made a little snorting noise. 'Maybe not in your wonderful old school full of liars but you seem pretty stupid here,' she said.

'Suit yourself,' I said. I hadn't even had breakfast yet and felt tired out.

Nothing much happened at breakfast. No talking allowed.

Left over from the days when the place had been a hotel, the beige-painted dining room had lots of little tables with six girls at each. Bernadette and I were together; the rest of the girls at our table were older and looked as though they wouldn't have wanted to talk to us anyway. As I glanced around the room a few people in my class stared me in an unfriendly manner. Except Chiquita, who sort of smiled.

There was only thick bread and red jam to eat with cups of tea. Apparently at the weekend we also got boiled eggs and fruit but anyway . . .

Straight afterwards I asked Sister Ita where I could find Sister Maria.

'I expect she'll be in her office, dear.'

She pointed to a door along the corridor from the dining room. It was a black painted door with a PRIVATE sign on it. This was going to be scary but I had to do something to save myself.

I knocked on the black door. There was a long pause then Sister Maria's low voice said, 'Come in.'

Sister Maria was sitting behind her desk, reading something. She kept reading even when I coughed to show I was there, but she obviously knew I was there because she'd said, 'Come in.' But she kept on reading...

Finally she lifted her head and looked at me with those cold grey eyes. 'Katherine. Did you want to speak to me?'

I took a deep brave-making breath and said, 'Yes, Sister. I have to explain something.'

She nodded. 'Go ahead, Katherine.'

So I told her about Chiquita Morris being upset and about my old school hating kids who owned up and knocking their blocks off.

She looked irritated and interrupted me. 'Katherine, this is a school for ladies. No one knocks blocks off here. Not for anything. And we encourage honesty in all things. Not owning up is like telling lies. Do you understand that?'

I nodded.

'But that was a kindness – to try to help Chiquita. I see you meant well there.'

I was going to say that I did but she held up her hand, not wanting me to speak.

Then she looked at me for a long time, deciding something.

'On reflection I have decided I won't telephone your home. Taking into consideration that you are from a very underprivileged background and have many things to learn, I think it would be fair to give you a chance to be with people who behave decently and properly. But I want to see clear evidence that you are learning to shake the habits of your background, Katherine. Go to class now, and don't disappoint me again for the entire length of your time at this school.'

I said thank you and got out of her office as fast as I could.

I didn't like all that talk about my background. It wasn't as if we had a fridge in the garden or I'd had a knife. But for now, feeling insulted probably wasn't the most important thing. It was more important that I'd not made a mistake out of a mistake. I had saved myself.

Next I had to save myself from the slight second mistake of how I'd managed to make everyone in my class hate me in a matter of one night.

There was no teacher in the classroom. Everyone was sitting whispering, except Chiquita Morris, who was looking at a magazine – not reading it, just flicking the pages, looking at the pictures. The whispering stopped when I came in.

'Well?' Bernadette asked as I sat down. I could see by her excited pointy little face she was waiting to gloat about the terrible punishment I'd be getting.

'She was OK,' I said, trying not to be too gloaty myself. 'She's let me off.'

Bernadette looked so shocked I might just as well have said I'd gone in the office and Sister Maria had been sitting there dressed as a sheep.

'What?' she gasped.

'What happened?' Danielle asked from behind us.

'Don't answer her,' Bernadette hissed at me.

'Was I asking you, Bernadette?' Danielle said, with superior sarcasm smeared all over her voice.

Bernadette twisted round to look at her with a 'so there' expression on her face. 'Sister Maria let her off.'

I looked back at Danielle. I hoped she would be annoyed, but she made a face like a holy saint.

'Oh, that's good,' she said all gushingly. 'Her reaction did seem rather over the top.'

'Over the top but your fault, though,' I said, and turned back to face the front.

Bernadette looked at me and actually almost smiled.

'Listen, Katherine...' Danielle was saying behind me. 'Excuse me, could you look at me when I'm talking to you...?'

I couldn't believe this girl with her attitude like she was the grown-up queen of the world. Whatever she wanted me to turn round for, I wasn't doing it.

'Excuse me, Katherine? I'm trying to talk to you.'

Bernadette turned round. 'She doesn't want to talk to you.'

Bernadette turned back to face the front and made a cross-eyed face to show me what she thought of Danielle. I agreed with the face. Who did Danielle think she was?

There was no chance to find out what kind of huge world queen she thought she was, because Sister Patricia bustled into the classroom carrying a pile of books and papers.

Everyone got to their feet, saying, 'Good morning, Sister Patricia.'

She made squeaky sound and said, 'Good morning, girls. Sit down, sit down.' There were drops of sweat on her face as if she'd run to class. Her brown veil was very crooked, sliding down one ear and showing spiky grey hair over her other ear.

Then she took some deep breaths to calm down, making her bosoms heave up and down like waves in the sea. She was hardly taller than us but had the most enormous bosoms. The crucifix around her neck was almost lying flat on the brown cloth shelf her bosoms made. She was so top-heavy it was amazing she didn't fall over.

Sister Patricia's bosoms were amazing but her lessons were not. So let's get on to interesting stuff that happened at break time. Recreation they called it. I suppose because it was a school where people paid money they had to call things by long names.

CHAPTER SEVEN

The fact that I had annoyed Danielle made me suddenly much less annoying to Bernadette. She smiled at me as we went outside and said, 'Come on, me and Fiona have to make a den every term. You and Sarah can help.'

I hadn't made a den since I was about six but I wasn't going to criticize or suggest it seemed childish. I needed to keep quiet and make friends.

Crossing the huge gardens we passed a fenced-in playground next to a newer building where the little kids of den-making age, under eleven, had their lessons. Only a few of them lived at the school; the rest had normal lives and went home at night to their families in the villages around the hills. The ones who lived at the school had rooms upstairs from ours, alongside the older girls so they'd have people to look after them. But that couldn't be the same as family to look after you.

Behind the little-kids building was a patch of trees with a fence at the back to show where the school grounds ended.

As we went into the patch of trees, Bernadette said we needed a 'headquarters' and she knew all about making dens because she had brothers. She said that as we were in a hurry we would just make a basic den, some tree branches piled on other tree branches to form a tunnel. She said that gradually we would make it 'more secure from prying eyes'. But for now, once we'd made a tunnel, we had to hurry and crawl inside.

Although it was quite a sunny day, once we were in the tunnel of leafy branches it felt almost cold and the light was eerily thin.

Bernadette looked serious and whispered, 'This is a den of utter secrecy. Anyone who tells anyone outside about the den has to go to the attic corridor and have their entrails pulled out by the mad nuns.'

'Mad nuns?' Sarah asked, looking like she'd cry.

'They keep them in the attic up a secret staircase beside the nuns' bedrooms,' Fiona said. 'They can't get out, Sarah. Don't worry.'

'How many are up there?' I asked, deciding I should keep a diary so I had all this sort of information ready in case of trouble.

'Three,' Bernadette said.

'Tell them,' Fiona said excitedly. 'Bernie explains it better than anyone. Danielle thinks she's an expert on the mad nuns because last term she said she'd done a dare to go into the nuns' part of the corridor but we knew she'd just pretended. She said she'd heard them make noises but Danielle is such a liar.'

Bernadette looked very pleased. 'Danielle doesn't even know the truth like I do. I know the full true stories because I was told by Ann Coyle when I was only seven, and Ann Coyle knew from her mother who'd been at this school and had really truthfully seen the mad nuns in the attic. And Ann Coyle's mother has had to take pills to stay calm ever since.'

I felt a bit impatient. 'So, are you going to tell us?' I asked, and Bernadette scowled at me.

'You can't be new and be told if you don't swear to secrecy.'

Me and Sarah swore. And I hoped it was going to be worth all this bossiness and fussing.

'OK, listen carefully because I have to talk quietly,' Bernadette said, and looked around as if she was checking for prying eyes. Then she put on a very good scary-story voice – slow, old ladyish and shaky, as if beads in her nose were rattling. 'About twenty years ago in this very convent, there was Sister Agnes, who was very beautiful but her parents had made her be a nun against her will. When she was here she met a man from the village who came to work on the new building.

'He was called Johnny. Sister Agnes tried to run away with Johnny but they caught her and made her go back to being a nun. She was so upset that once, in the middle of the night, she went out to the roof of the new building where Johnny had worked. She cried out his name and then flung herself to the ground. She didn't die but she broke her leg, squashed all her beautiful face and one of her eyes came out. So now she's gone mad and they keep her in the attic. Sometimes, if any builders or people like that come to the school, you hear her screaming, "Johnny! Johnny!" Screaming, screaming with tears pouring from one eye and running down her crushed face and nothing at all in the empty eye but dust.'

Sarah looked as if she was going to start screaming and screaming. I don't know what I looked like – hopefully just cool about it. Like Fiona looked. But then she had heard all this before.

Sarah controlled herself enough to ask, 'What happened to Johnny?'

'Oh, he went off and married someone who wasn't a nun. He didn't care – men are like that. Anyway, he's not important,' Bernadette said, a bit irritated with the question.

I agreed. Who cared about Johnny? Crushed-faced eyeless nuns were the important thing. I was so surprised Bernadette could tell stories like this. And she had stood up for me against Danielle. Surprises on surprises.

'Tell them about the others,' Fiona urged Bernadette. 'The other two are even better.'

Bernadette looked smug for a moment, obviously showing off inside her own head about how talented she was at storytelling. Eventually she took a deep breath, said, 'All right then,' and started telling the story in her ordinary voice.

'Well, then there is Sister Benedict. She worked in the convent in India. She's the sister of Sister Vincent, who teaches music and netball and stuff. You'll hear Sister Vincent go on and on about India and how the girls there are really poor but well-behaved and not like us. Sister Vincent would much rather be back in India but she has to be here because of Sister Benedict, who has leprosy that she caught from poor lepers in India.'

At this point, Bernadette took a deep breath and looked at each of us in turn, as if to make sure we were really listening. Then she returned to using her scary voice.

'Sister Benedict's hands are almost completely eaten away with leprosy and she only has two toes. A big toe on her left foot and a little toe on her right foot. She walks like a monstrous ape balancing on a tightrope. Her nose is all gone so you can see right through to her brain. Her tongue has entirely gone so she can't talk. She just makes a noise like, "Shnerguh, shnerguh," and coughs up black phlegm. They have to feed her through a slot in the door with a long spoon. They daren't open the door, or she'll try and get out and give everyone leprosy out of spite. The only person who can go in, or catch her if she escapes, is Sister Vincent because sisters can't catch leprosy from each other. So Sister Vincent has to stay here just in case. Sometimes, in the night, you can hear Sister Benedict coughing black phlegm and going, "Shnerguh, shnerguh." The nuns will tell you it's foxes in the woods but that's a lie.'

'I don't want to hear any more,' Sarah said.

'It's just stories,' I said.

'No, it's not,' Bernadette said crossly. 'It's true.'

Sarah let out a wail and crashed out of the den, nearly wrecking it.

Fiona said, 'Oh dear, Bernie, I better go after her in case she tells.'

Bernadette showed her true mean self, saying, 'New girls are so stupid.'

I was going to say I wasn't stupid but realized it would be wasting time arguing when there was another story.

'What's the third story?' I asked quickly.

'I'll only tell you if you swear to believe it's true,' Bernadette said.

I swore to believe it was true.

Fiona said, 'You know I believe it, Bernie, but we should look for Sarah.'

'Yes, yes, in a minute,' Bernadette said, and fiddled with some branches, so we were properly covered up again.

I thought time was going to be wasted in an argument between Fiona and Bernadette, but Sarah reappeared. She sat at the edge of the den and said, 'Sorry about that.'

'She's going to tell another story,' Fiona said. 'Will you be OK?'

Sarah nodded, forcing herself to be brave.

'All right then,' Bernadette said, after a glare at Sarah.

'Lastly there is Sister Frances. And get ready to be shocked, because Sister Frances got pregnant by a priest. Not Father Malone who comes here now but an Italian priest who visited called Father Louis. Sister Frances was really scared, so she sold her soul to the devil so she wouldn't be pregnant any more. And it worked. Father Louis went back to Italy to work for the Pope and by a hellish miracle Sister Frances wasn't pregnant any more. She relaxed and went about her business teaching the fifth form, very relieved that her stupid sluttishness with Father Louis hadn't got her into trouble.

'But then one terrible night, exactly a year later, Satan came to her in her bedroom and said, "Remember, I will have your soul when you die and you will be tortured eternally in the fires of hell." Then Satan vanished in a puff of sewer-stinking smoke. Gazing upon the face of Satan and realizing the terrible thing she had done sent Sister Frances totally screaming mad on the spot. To this day she keeps screaming, "I want to change my mind, I want to have my baby!" And if she gets out she runs into the villages and farmhouses, trying to grab babies and accidentally strangles them she hugs them so tight.'

We all sat very still for a moment.

'There,' Fiona said eventually. 'Now do you believe her?'

I didn't see that Bernadette had given us any actual proof but she definitely knew how to tell a story.

I was so glad I'd found something good about Bernadette. If I was going to be with her and her complaining meanness morning, noon and night, it might make her bearable. I wanted to suggest a plan to try and see the mad nuns but the bell rang for playtime – recreation – to be over before I had a chance to speak.

CHAPTER EIGHT

We passed Danielle and her crowd sitting in the sun, plaiting each other's hair and talking about pop stars.

'Where have you lot been?' Danielle made a superior type of face. 'You're all filthy dirty. Surely you've grown out of making dens by now, Bernadette.'

'You think you're cool but you're just boring,' Bernadette said.

Danielle made a cool, mature type of laugh. 'Oh really, how pathetic,' she said to her crowd.

For a moment I felt embarrassed to be in the den crowd, not Danielle's sophisticated crowd. But then I realized I would far rather have heard the mad-nun stories in the den than be plaiting hair and listening to Danielle saying, 'No, I'll tell you why you shouldn't like him any more…' Maybe dens was something not very cool or anything, but it was better than hair and blah-blah arguments about what pop stars were best – always pointless arguments because people were crazy adamant about the people they liked and there was no changing their mind.

Maybe Danielle and her friends were the cool ones in our class but I'd never been one of the cool ones at my old school either. I'd always had friends who were slightly weird but interesting. Part of me wanted to be cool and sophisticated but it never seemed to happen. Mum would buy me good clothes and CDs whenever she could afford it – but there was obviously some extra secret ingredient to coolness I didn't have, because owning these things didn't change how I was. I was one of the weird ones whatever I wore or owned. As if inner weirdness must show in my face. It didn't matter – no one cool ever solved crimes or had to fight a completely insane locked-up nun.

Chiquita Morris, on the other hand, looked sort of cool even though she was obviously full of inner weirdness. She sat on a bench in the gardens away from everyone else, flicking through glossy magazines. There was something about the way she didn't care what anyone thought about her that was very cool. She was cut off in a world of her own and I wondered what went on in her secret world.

Unfortunately, as I went up the steps into school with Bernadette, Sarah and Fiona, we were laughing loudly because we'd been making the noise like Sister Benedict: 'Shnurguh, shnurguh, shnurguh!' Chiquita was walking towards us. She looked at me as if I was a leprous thing she couldn't bear to see and I realized too late she might have thought we were laughing at her.

After that, I lost track of her for a few days. It was busy, all new lessons such as French and chemistry and things I'd never learned before. Every one of these confusing lessons had homework.

I was rubbish at their sports – hockey and netball. I'd never been good at netball and hit myself on the head with my hockey stick the first time I tried playing that.

Bernadette was the opposite – unconfused by all lessons, and captain of hockey and netball. Some people might have been surprised to hear that Bernadette was the captain because Danielle acted as if she was in charge – always telling people to 'buck up', as if she came from one of those very old-fashioned boarding-school books I'd read, where girls thought things were 'jolly' and the worst swearing they knew was 'yipes!'

If you watched Danielle carefully, she did this shouting and ran around very busily, but never really scored goals or did anything actually useful. She just had a knack of seeming to be important on the hockey pitch or netball court – the way she had a knack of seeming to be very important in life.

She was always in the centre of things, chattering and laughing – drawing people into her cheerful light, like the sun. Whereas Bernadette was a scrunched-up, freckly, wee-smelling magnet for the handful of people who didn't like Danielle, or were too unimportant for Danielle to notice. I was stuck with the magnet rather than the sun but, after that first night, I knew I could never like Danielle again. To me, Danielle's sunshininess was like a too-hot day that made you feel itchy and scratchy – and like you might get burned.

Bernadette was rude and bad-tempered but she wasn't complicated to deal with. Danielle, on the other hand...

I think it was the third night at school, on the way back from the toilet – lavatory – when Danielle came up to me on the landing, holding out her hand to shake hands and smiling her warmest smile. 'I feel we made a bad start, Katherine, but let's try and put that right.'

I shook her hand and nodded. But inside my head I was thinking, *You do think you're some kind of queen of the world, you do!*

'Anyway,' she went on to say, as if I was the person she most wanted to be friends with of anyone she had ever met, 'a word of advice, Katherine. Your roommate, Bernadette, is not trusted by many people in this school.'

I asked her what she meant.

'Well, there were a several thefts last term and I'm afraid a lot of evidence pointed to her.' She smiled as if she knew everything in the universe. 'Just so you're careful about your pocket money and valuable belongings around her, Katherine. It may not be her. I'm working on the evidence but in the meantime, best to be careful.'

'What evidence?' I asked her. This was a nightmare. Danielle with evidence on crimes?

She laughed as if she was slightly embarrassed. 'That's rather secret until I'm sure of my facts. But I do read a great many detective books, so I've a very good idea about these things. Anyway, I just thought you should be warned.' And she went off down the corridor with a flick of her blonde plait and her dark blue possibly silk dressing gown swishing.

I felt as if she'd smarmily crept into my brain and stolen my life.

I couldn't bear it that Danielle seemed to have put herself in charge of solving crimes as well as everything else. It was a sick-making horror to hear her say she knew detective matters. And I didn't believe her. It was a bit too obvious that Bernadette, her arch-enemy, was the one she suspected most of crimes.

It seemed to me that I might be collecting evidence that Danielle was a massive liar as well as a smiling, laughing snitch.

'When collecting evidence,' Grandad always said, 'it's better to listen and watch more than you speak.'

So I said nothing to Bernadette. Not a word to anyone.

CHAPTER NINE

I wrote to Mum about simple things, such as what new lessons I had – I definitely didn't tell her about the nuns in the attic. I had a feeling it would make her take me away from the school – mad nuns probably being in the area of the kind of weird thing she was afraid of from nuns.

Grandad, on the other hand, would have been very happy to get my letter to him, full of the tales of mad nuns and rumours of crime.

I told them both that me and Bernadette had become great friends, which wasn't really true but the situation had improved since the stories and both not liking Danielle.

The situation with Chiquita Morris had disimproved. She ignored me now when I said hello. It wasn't as if she had a choice of people to say hello to. I always saw her sitting around alone, looking at magazines and eating chocolate, crisps or sweets by the fistful. She was one of those people who chewed with her mouth wide open so you could see all the slush going around, which was a bit off-putting.

But not enough for the real spite Bernadette had against her, which I didn't understand at all. It wasn't as if Chiquita argued with her like Danielle did, but any chance she had, Bernadette said something horrible about Chiquita.

I asked Bernadette what exactly Chiquita had done wrong to her – all Chiquita did was mind her own business and read magazines.

'Oh, that reading magazines is a new thing this term. She used to just sit staring into space – don't you think that's peculiar? Well, I do and I don't like her.'

This didn't seem like a good reason but it was tiring to try and figure out how these boarding-school girls thought about things. I was exhausted with all the newness and found it hard to drag myself out of bed when the bell went at seven. I was exhausted but at night I'd lie awake for ages with everything flying around in my brain.

At eight o'clock, when the lights went out, there was the usual no-talking rule but sometimes Bernadette would talk to me in whispers. Usually she'd rabbit on about hating everything, but one night she started to tell me interesting things about foreign places she'd lived – Indonesia, Japan and Hong Kong. Apart from school, Bernadette and her brothers had never lived in England their whole lives. And her dad was Irish. Like my grandad. We made each other laugh doing Irish accents and yet again I found a surprisingly good side of Bernadette.

After we'd got bored doing Irish accents, we lay awake talking about how it would be much better if the nuns let us stay up to watch television instead of sending us to bed so early. The nuns only let us watch television on Saturdays, apparently, and I agreed with Bernadette that this was peculiar. Then Bernadette really surprised me and said, 'Hey, want to do a dare?'

I said of course I did.

'Let's sneak into the nuns' quarters and see what it's like.'

'Won't they be in there?'

'No, they have their supper and prayers now. If we get caught it will be horrific but no one in this year has dared do it. Danielle said she did but she didn't show any proof. Lillian Green in the year above did it last year and stole Sister Patricia's veil as proof.'

'So, we'll steal a veil?'

'Well, we have to be careful – this is a very dangerous dare.'

'I know,' I said. 'But if we could go and get proof we'd been, that would make Danielle look pretty dumb.' I knew this would make Bernadette want to go through with it.

'OK,' she said. 'Let's just practise for now. Let's just go through the door to their section and see what it looks like. Then once we've worked out how to get around, let's really explore and get proof.'

'Right,' I said, getting out of bed and trying to find my slippers with my feet. 'And what about the attic?'

Bernadette didn't say anything for a minute. 'Well,' she whispered in her scary-story voice, 'maybe we can see if it's true about the third staircase.' Apparently Danielle and

Lillian Green both said that they'd seen the secret third staircase.

As well as the private nuns' stairs and the front stairs that pupils used, there was this third staircase with a metal barred gate on it, starting on the first-floor nuns' quarters and leading up to the attic full of the mad ones. Danielle had claimed she'd heard noises coming from the mad nuns. Even if we didn't get to hear noises or pinch a veil or anything as proof, we could see the third staircase for ourselves.

'We might see the mad nuns' hands clawing through the barred gate,' Bernadette whispered. Then we decided we'd better not say anything more about this for now or we'd get too scared to go.

CHAPTER TEN

We crept along the darkened first-floor landing towards the forbidden door to the nuns' quarters. From the girls' rooms we could hear whispers, occasional giggling. There was no sign of Sister Ita, who Bernadette said sometimes crept up the front stairs and pounced into rooms where she heard talking.

We passed the last of the girls' bedrooms, no more comforting sounds of whispering. The corridor was darker. This was an old building, remember, so every step we took seemed to make a floorboard creak under the lino.

There was a green glowing light over the forbidden door that read: FIRE EXIT. Another sign on it said: NO PUPILS PAST THIS POINT, EXCEPT IN EMERGENCY. Maybe if we were caught we could pretend we thought there was a fire...

It occurred to me that I could smell Bernadette. Any nun that might jump out and nearly catch us would know by the evidence of her own nose that the girl she thought she'd seen out of the corner of her eye must surely have been Bernadette. Still, Bernadette had started this dare, so she must know the extra risk she was taking with her tell-tale smell.

Bernadette peered through the glass in the nuns' door. 'Can't see anyone,' she whispered.

I pushed the door on my side. It was heavy but moved silently. Bernadette slipped through the gap, smelling a lot now, possibly due to nerves. I followed, holding the door so it wouldn't bang closed.

The nuns' side looked like our side: dim corridor lights and lots of doors. No lights came from under the doors. At the end there was a door marked BATHROOM. We crept towards this, hardly daring to breathe. To the right, the corridor went towards the nuns' private stairs and another door marked BATHROOM. Bernadette clutched my arm. There, just beside the first bathroom, in a little alcove, was a metal grille with some tiny wooden stairs behind it. And the metal grille was slightly open – a broken padlock hanging off it!

Suddenly we heard a noise from one of the nuns' rooms. A door opening. Bernadette squeaked and ran back towards the fire door. I thought she was crazy, she'd be seen for sure. I took two big strides into the nearest room, the bathroom. There were heavy curtains on the window. I could get in behind those just in time...

Just in time before what? A mad Agnes with no eye, Frances with no soul, or leprosy-spreading Benedict came in looking for victims?

I stood behind the thick curtains with terrifying ideas racing in my head. Sister Benedict would be the worst one to have got out, limping around trying to kill everyone with leprosy. What if she had already been down the corridor to the nuns' part of the building, killed all the nuns and now she was backtracking to kill all the girls?

The first person she would be likely to kill would be Bernadette because she'd track her by the smell; even Benedict with no nose and only an exposed sniffing brain would smell Bernadette before she smelled me. Poor Bernadette would be the first person to be killed... No. The first person to be killed would be me because someone was coming into the bathroom and turning the light on!

I could see the bath through the gap in the curtains. Hanging on a washing line over the bath was the most enormous bra, like something made by the army. I had no time to think about enormous bras – something was shuffling across the room.

Probably Benedict, the worst of the mad nuns, who would pull back the curtains, sniff through no nose and give me leprosy.

Then I saw a blue fluffy sleeve reach out and take down the enormous bra. A small form bent over to put the plug in the bath and turn the taps on. It was Sister Patricia.

I nearly jumped out and said, 'Thank goodness you're safe, we have to run for our lives – the metal gate is open!'

But something made me think about the word 'imagination'. How imagination could get you completely carried away to be scared of things that didn't exist. When really perhaps you should be scared of the real thing in front of you – a nun in a blue fluffy dressing gown holding her enormous bra. A nun with a bra who might find you behind the curtains of her bathroom at any moment.

In some ways Benedict with leprosy would be better. At least I couldn't be blamed for that. In fact I could have maybe strangled Benedict with the enormous bra and saved the day. But now...Now Sister Patricia was humming a hymn and moving around the room. *Please don't let her decide to look out of the window for some reason. Please let me just become invisible and waft invisibly back to my room . . .*

The water was gushing into the bath. Soon it would be ready and, more terrible than any kind of nose-eating disease, at any moment I was going to see Sister Patricia completely naked.

A nun in the nude would surely be massive trouble and I'd be expelled and probably sent to hell with Satan when I died.

Sister Patricia finding me now, before she took off her robe, would be bad – I'd already seen her enormous bra and the short spiky hair she had without her veil on. But if she found me after she'd had the bath...After she'd been relaxing, all completely nude enormous-bosomed nun in the bath...I had to move now, this instant.

I coughed and stepped out from behind the curtains.

Sister Patricia squeaked with fright and clutched her robe around her. 'Katherine Milne. What are you doing?'

'Hide-and-seek, Sister,' I said quickly, thinking it might be a good excuse.

'But you're not allowed in this part of the corridor,' she said, face all red. She kept one hand holding her robe and moved the other behind her back, to hide the enormous bra.

'I got confused,' I said. 'Sorry, Sister.'

Now she'd got over her fright at seeing me, Sister Patricia was furious. 'Confused, my foot!' she said. 'How dare you be in our bathroom. What sort of trouble do you want to get into?'

'I don't want to get into trouble,' I said. 'I am sorry.'

'Sorry won't do,' she said, after a very angry squeak.

I thought she might beat my brains out with the bra but I remembered something that might save me.

'Sister Patricia, do you know the metal gate is open?'

'What?' She looked shocked.

'The metal gate to the attic staircase.'

'Follow me, Katherine,' she said, and scurried outside. She looked at the metal gate, then looked up the wooden staircase and seemed completely horrified. She put her little fat hand in the pocket of her bathrobe, pulled out a mobile phone, pressed a number and said, 'Sister Vincent, you'd better come up to our sleeping quarters immediately.'

She put the phone back in her pocket and looked at the broken padlock on the metal gate, making distressed squeaking noises.

'Go to your room and go to sleep, Katherine. I've no time to deal with you now. Go on, go.'

I went as fast as I could. As I went through the fire door I glanced back at Sister Patricia pacing to and fro by the metal door. She was pressing another phone number with one hand and rubbing at her spiky hair with her other hand like someone going crazy with fear and worry.

CHAPTER ELEVEN

Bernadette was sitting up in bed, looking as if she was ready to cover her head with the duvet at any moment.

'What happened?'

'Sister Patricia caught me.'

'What did she say? You'll be in real trouble this time.'

'She doesn't care about me, not now she knows the metal gate is open.'

'What?'

'There is something up there. Sister Patricia saw the gate was open, immediately got all frantic and called Sister Vincent.'

'Sister Vincent. That means Sister Benedict is out. The worst of all.'

Then Bernadette told me to be quiet, to see if we could hear the 'Shnurguh, shnurguh'.

I couldn't stand to be just listening for the worst. I told Bernadette how I'd seen Sister Patricia's horrified face; it wasn't all stories and imagination. Sister Patricia was horrified for real.

'We should tell everyone,' I blurted out in a panic. 'We should all get in one room furthest away from the nuns' quarters and barricade the door.'

'I don't think—' Bernadette started to say.

'Quickly,' I said. 'Don't even get your slippers or anything, there's no time.' This was going to be so great – people needed saving and I had a plan.

We ran into the corridor and into the first room, which was Fiona and Sarah's. We shook them awake.

'Sister Benedict might have got out,' I said. 'Quick, run!'

Fiona said, 'What?' Sarah just screamed. Screamed so loud anyone in the world with leprosy could have heard her.

'Shut up!' Bernadette hissed at her. 'She'll hear you. Shut up!'

I grabbed Sarah by the arm and pulled her out of the room and into the next one. She was sobbing, but at least had the sense to stop screaming and bringing Benedict and maybe the others rushing down on us.

As we ran from room to room, shaking girls awake, telling them to leave their slippers and just run, I kept glancing back up the corridor. I expected some terrible sight of mouldy nunnery on two toes, followed by squashed-faced one-eyed strangling horrors, to be bursting through the fire doors . . . But so far we were ahead of them.

There was a big crowd following us now as we burst into the last room – Danielle's. Indira and Danielle were already awake as they'd heard the screaming and running feet.

'What's going on?' Danielle demanded as I directed every girl in our class into her room.

'Hang on,' Bernadette said. 'We forgot Chiquita.'

Chiquita had a little room on her own opposite Danielle's. Bernadette started to go out but she was struggling against the crowd of frightened girls coming into Danielle's room.

'Stop right there!' Danielle ordered. 'All of you stop coming into my room and tell me what's going on!'

'Benedict's out, all of them are out,' I said, and rushed to help Bernadette.

It was surprising Bernadette wanted to save Chiquita, who she hated so much, but I suppose it showed Bernadette was kind in an emergency.

Chiquita's room was tiny, more like a little cupboard. By the light from the corridor we could see there was no one in the bed.

'Look!' Bernadette said.

Things were thrown all around the room. And no sign of Chiquita.

'They've got her!' Bernadette yelped. 'They're nearby!' We ran back across the corridor and into Danielle's very crowded room.

'Make a barricade!' Bernadette shouted as she shut the door.

I started to push the dressing table in front of the door; Sarah and Fiona helped me. Girls were whispering, whimpering and huddling up to each other all around the room. I felt I should probably say something to make them feel brave. I had got everyone in a complete frenzy and it was up to me to make them brave and tell them more plans – but I wasn't sure I had any more plans after the dressing table. Suddenly Danielle jumped on her bed and clapped her hands.

'Listen! Listen to me! Why are you all in here? Whose idea was this?'

'Shut up, Danielle. They've already got Chiquita,' Bernadette said. 'We have to get everyone in one room and make it secure.'

I was livid that Danielle was putting herself in charge while I was still thinking of new plans and things to say. I had to make her shut up and be scared so she wouldn't spoil everything.

'The metal gate was open,' I said. 'Sister Patricia phoned for Sister Vincent.'

'Right,' Danielle said, getting down off her bed. 'Let's calm down and do this properly. That dressing table's not heavy enough. Someone move the wardrobe. No, wait, what about all the girls upstairs, what about them? I better go and warn them.'

'You stupid idiot, you can't go out there!' Bernadette shouted at her. 'They've already got Chiquita.'

Danielle stopped moving towards the door. I was pleased about this because the way she was trying to take over being the one to rescue everyone was making me crazy.

'Right, you're right, we shouldn't open this door,'

Danielle said. 'But I have a plan. Let's shout out of the windows to warn them.'

This was going to be quite hard because the windows had those locks that meant you could only open them a certain amount.

'Come on!' Danielle bossed. 'Some of you go and shout out of the window – shout upwards – some of you move the wardrobe and I'll think what to do next. Come on!' She was snapping her fingers as if she could do some kind of magic trick. Nobody moved to do her orders. By this stage I think everyone was too scared to move.

Then they got even more scared because something started trying to smash the door open, banging it against the dressing table.

Something was trying to get in!

A few girls screamed. Me and Bernadette leaned against the dressing table.

'I told you it wasn't heavy enough!' Danielle shouted, dancing up and down, stamping her feet in the middle of the room and being completely useless.

Some other girls realized what we were doing and helped push the dressing table against the door so it was kept shut.

Whatever was outside started hammering on the door. More girls screamed. More hammering. The screaming was like police sirens now.

Then Bernadette shouted, 'Shut up, everyone! Listen!'

When everyone's screaming stopped and whimpered

down to crying, we could hear the banging. And hear Sister Ita's voice shouting, 'What on earth is going on? Open the door this instant! Open this door!'

We moved away from the dressing table.

'It's Sister Ita, you idiots,' Danielle said, moving towards the door.

'Wait,' I said. 'What if it's a trick and they're holding on to her to make her say that, then they'll get us.'

Danielle shoved me out of the way and started pulling the dressing table.

'Help me,' she said to some of the others. 'This idiot's got us all in deep trouble.'

No one helped her at first, then some Danielle fans shoved the dressing table with her. The door flew open, the light came on and there was Sister Ita, out of breath and furious.

'Sister Maria is on her way up here. Now will somebody mind telling me what is going on?'

Nobody said anything but Danielle looked at me. Obviously she was thinking she might get some new chance to snitch.

The word 'imagination' was starting to come into my head again. But no, I still had the fact that the gate had been open and Sister Patricia had panicked.

'It was to keep us safe,' I said. 'The metal gate was open.'

'The metal gate?' Sister Ita looked like she'd never heard of such a thing. And her face was now as pink as a baboon's bottom.

'I thought the attic nuns were out,' I said.

Sister Ita's baboon-bottom face stared as if I was the one with an animal's rear-end face. 'What?' she asked me. 'Is this some sort of game?'

'It wasn't a game,' Bernadette said. 'Sister Patricia called Sister Vincent about the gate and Chiquita's missing. Her room's all wrecked.'

Sister Ita looked around at everyone. She looked less angry now, and more confused.

'All go back to bed immediately,' she said. Then she pointed at me and Bernadette. 'You two come along to your room with me and have a little talk.'

As I followed Sister Ita out of the room, Danielle smiled at me in a way I could see was a silent way of laughing at me.

Sister Ita waited until we were back in our room before she turned on us. 'So,' she said, 'you have woken the whole school and caused chaos. Would you mind giving me your reasons?'

Bernadette looked as if she was trying to think of the reasons. But we had perfectly good reasons.

'Chiquita's missing,' I said. 'Her room's wrecked.'

'Chiquita's no concern of yours,' Sister Ita said sharply. 'And that doesn't explain why you caused this general panic. What was this nonsense about the metal gate?'

'It was open,' I said. 'Ask Sister Patricia.'

'How did you know it was open?' Sister Ita's eyes narrowed as if to warn me there was no point lying.

'I went up there for a dare,' I said quietly.

'Me too,' Bernadette said bravely.

'But it was mainly me,' I said, because it did seem to be mainly me that had caused all this.

Sister Ita thought for a moment, then made a tutting sound before she asked, 'Is this something to do with nuns in the attic?'

I was so relieved – at least she knew why I'd had to try and save everyone. 'Yes, Sister, I thought they'd got out.'

Sister Ita looked at Bernadette, then back at me.

'There is nothing in the attic,' she said. 'Who told you there was?'

'Everyone says,' I said, trying to save Bernadette. But true to the kamikaze owning-up policy, she owned up.

'I told her,' she said.

'Haven't you been in trouble for spreading those old stories before?'

Bernadette nodded. 'Last year, Sister,' she said.

And then, just when I thought it probably was all old stories of Bernadette's and I hadn't any evidence for anything I'd done except in my own imagination, we heard terrible screaming from the nuns' end of the corridor.

Sister Ita held up her hand to keep us quiet and listened. 'Chiquita,' she muttered, and hurried out of our room, saying quickly over her shoulder, 'Go to bed. This is nothing for you to worry about.'

And she turned our light out, leaving us standing there in the dark, listening to her running feet and the sound of Chiquita screaming.

CHAPTER TWELVE

We sat on our beds in the dark. There didn't seem to be any point whispering. Who was going to tell us off for talking after everything that had gone on?

'Are you scared?' Bernadette asked.

I was less scared now that Chiquita had stopped screaming. I was beginning to feel more confused than anything else.

'Do you know what's going on?' I asked – I don't know why I thought Bernadette would know more than me but there was a tiny chance she might.

'I'm trying to figure it out,' she said.

'Yes,' I said. 'We should maybe try and figure it out and take away any parts of it that we might have imagined. Chiquita missing and now screaming. We didn't imagine that.'

'What did we imagine then?' Bernadette asked.

'The nuns in the attic getting out. I mean we didn't actually see them. Just the gate open.'

'You said Sister Patricia phoned Sister Vincent. She's

supposed to be the one who can control Sister Benedict and stop her spreading leprosy. And where did Sister Ita run off to if she wasn't helping rescue Chiquita from mad nuns?'

These were all very good points Bernadette was making. I was pleased. It wasn't just my imagination. I turned my thoughts to the evidence and found an interesting question to ask: 'Why would the mad nuns come all the way down the corridor and only take Chiquita?'

'I don't know,' Bernadette said. 'Maybe she's the one they know best seeing as she's always here. Maybe she goes to the metal gate when it's quiet in the holidays and teases them. And now they're taking their revenge.'

'That's good,' I said. 'That's a very good reason. Do you think they really are there then, Bernadette? Truthfully, tell me.'

Bernadette suddenly stopped being interesting and sounded cross and bossy. 'I don't know. People have talked about it for years. I'm tired now. We don't know anything, we're just talking for the sake of it and I'm tired. Maybe the nuns will tell us about it in the morning.'

'Maybe they won't. Maybe if something has happened to Chiquita they'll cover up the story to save the school. If one of their pupils was strangled or killed of leprosy and it was their fault, they'd be ruined. I don't think they will tell us a single thing.'

'I can't think straight,' Bernadette said. I could hear her getting under her duvet. 'I feel cold now and tired. Let's see what happens in the morning.'

Bernadette had been great in the adventure so far; it was very disappointing that all she wanted now was sleep.

'The morning might be too late.'

'I don't see why,' Bernadette said, yawning.

'We could still be in danger from the attic,' I said, getting to my feet and walking to the door to show her I was still ready to do more things.

'I'm going to creep up the corridor and see what's happening through the nuns' door,' I said, going to open our bedroom door.

'Don't,' Bernadette said. 'You'll be in so much trouble. You're crazy.'

I did let out the squeal of a crazy person right then because our door suddenly opened just as I touched it and Danielle hurried in.

'Quiet,' she said. 'It's only me.'

'You gave me a fright,' I said, out of breath from the shock.

'I had to find out what was going on,' Danielle said. 'Did you hear Chiquita screaming? What did Sister Ita say to you?'

'Nothing,' I said. 'She just ran to see what was happening with Chiquita.'

'I see,' Danielle said, closing the door behind her. 'Right, I think we should backtrack. What exactly happened here? Explain it to me, right from the beginning.'

I couldn't stand her 'I'm in charge even if I wasn't there'

tone of voice. Why should we tell her anything? Why not just punch her in the head?

'It's a long story,' I said.

'We're going to sleep,' Bernadette grumbled from under her duvet.

'Yes,' I said. 'We're very tired now, we're going to sleep.'

'You were going out of your room,' Danielle said.

'I needed the toilet,' I said.

'Good idea,' Danielle said. 'We can say we're going to the lavatory and then take a look through the fire door and see what's happening in the nuns' corridor.'

'Maybe nothing's happening,' I said, to keep her from taking over the adventure.

'I doubt that,' she said. 'Come on. Let's take a look.'

Bernadette made a cross grunting sound from under her duvet.

'What's the matter, Bernadette, too scared?' Danielle said, with a little false laugh.

'She's not scared, she's tired,' I said. 'And, anyway, why don't you tell us what you know about the attic? Aren't you supposed to have heard noises?'

'Of course I did,' Danielle said indignantly. 'I went up to the metal gate and heard noises behind it, definite noises.'

'Hah! That's such a lie,' Bernadette said loudly, suddenly sounding very awake.

'We're wasting time,' Danielle said crossly. She opened the door and even though I didn't want to be on an adventure with her I had to follow.

Out in the corridor, heading towards us, was Sister Ita. There was no time to duck back into the room.

'Danielle Kirkham-Byles, what do you think you're doing in that room? And, you, what are you doing running about again?'

Sister Ita looked tired and upset more than angry with us.

'I simply wanted to know what was going on,' Danielle said, as if she was in charge of Sister Ita and the whole universe.

'It's none of your business, young lady,' Sister Ita said. 'Go to your room and go to sleep.'

'I know we shouldn't be out of bed, Sister,' Danielle said, niceness oozing out of her like treacle, 'but we are all very concerned about Chiquita.'

'Or are you just plain nosy, Danielle?' Sister Ita said sharply, making herself my favourite nun regardless of any other angry baboonishness she ever did again.

Danielle looked highly insulted and said, 'Very well. In that case, Sister, I'll go to bed and worry about Chiquita all night.' She started to walk away, nose in the air.

Sister Ita snapped at her, 'You needn't make a big drama out of it, Danielle. Chiquita Morris is in the infirmary and should be back in class tomorrow.'

Danielle turned to look at Sister Ita like an empress looking at an ant. 'Thank you, Sister,' she said. 'I was simply concerned about my friend.'

Then she flounced off to her room. Sister Ita shook her

head wearily, muttering to herself, 'Little madam.' Then she turned to me. 'Are you still here?'

'Um, yes. Shall I go to bed?'

'Yes, I think you'd better.'

I went to bed double fast in case she remembered she ought to tell me off a bit more.

'Chiquita's in the infirmary?' Bernadette asked sleepily when I went back into our room.

'Yes,' I said. 'What does that mean?'

'Mauled maybe,' Bernadette said. 'Strangled or bitten.' And then she fell asleep, snoring, leaving me with my head full of wild ideas, staring at the ceiling and sure I could hear, somewhere in the far distance, an echoing faint sound of 'Shnurguh, shnurguh!'

CHAPTER THIRTEEN

The infirmary was in the newer building, where the little kids had their classrooms. And some nuns lived there, so we had to be really careful.

Consisting of two bedrooms, the infirmary was for girls who were a bit sick, but not sick enough for hospital or being sent home. There was also a sort of doctor's room. Every morning at nine, except Sundays, Sister Vincent was there for girls who thought they were ill. Bernadette said she gave you an aspirin for everything, even if your head fell off. But she was supposed to be some kind of doctor.

Bernadette had woken up with a very good plan and we were doing it.

The bell to get up had gone at seven. Sister Ita had checked everyone was out of bed and said to us, 'Sister Maria wants to see you pair in her office before school.' Then she waited in the doorway a moment, arms folded, before she added, 'Move faster than that. If you're feeling tired you've no one to blame but yourselves.'

When she'd gone we'd moved very fast, too busy with our plan to think about tiredness. We'd got dressed and made our beds double quick. We would only have a short time to sneak downstairs, creep out of the side door, run along the side of the garden to the new building, sneak up to the infirmary, find out about Chiquita and be back upstairs to line up in time for breakfast. About fifteen minutes at the most.

So far it was going fine and we'd managed to get right outside the infirmary with no one seeing us. In a small, blue room, Chiquita was asleep. She didn't look hideously mauled and seemed to still have a nose and two eyes.

We decided we had to wake her up. This took quite a lot of shaking.

'Get off,' she grumbled at us.

'Chiquita? Are you OK?' Bernadette asked her.

'Get lost,' Chiquita said.

'What happened?' I asked her.

'Get lost,' she said again, and turned her back on us, curling up as if she was going to sleep.

'Did a mad nun get you?' Bernadette asked her.

Chiquita rolled back and looked at her. 'You are so stupid,' she said. 'So totally stupid and you stink. Why don't you get lost, you and your stupid new girl.'

I realized I didn't know Chiquita. All I'd seen was crying, or glamorous lonely Chiquita. Not this vicious Chiquita.

'Oh, typical,' Bernadette said. 'We were worried about you. There's no need to be like that.'

'Get lost!' Chiquita yelled at her. She sat up in bed and yelled even louder. 'Get lost!'

At that point we took the hint and did get lost, running out of the room and out of the new block as fast as we could, before her yelling brought nuns.

We were just in time to line up for breakfast, and then, annoyingly, there was no talking at breakfast. We only had a chance to talk while we waited outside Sister Maria's office.

'At least we know she's not hurt,' I said. 'Even though she must be a bit ill.'

'I hope she is ill,' Bernadette said. 'I hope she's got the beginnings of leprosy and that's why she's there. By tonight they'll send her away to a leper colony to rot.'

I didn't know what the beginnings of leprosy looked like and I didn't think Bernadette did either. But I was pretty sure that there must be more to it than being in a massively bad temper and yelling 'Get lost!' all the time.

'I don't see why she was so angry with us,' I said.

'You don't know her.' Bernadette made her disgusted face. 'She's spoilt and selfish and common as dirt and completely disgusting.'

'I still want to know what happened,' I said. 'Even if Chiquita is all those things.'

'Me too,' Bernadette said thoughtfully. 'I'll get raging leprosy myself from sheer nosiness if I never find out.'

I thought this was quite funny. What a surprise if

Bernadette turned out to be funny as well as really quite interesting under all her meanness.

'I'm sure you were told to wait here in silence,' Sister Maria said, coming up behind us all of a sudden. She pulled a big bunch of keys from a chain on her belt and unlocked her office door. Any feeling we had of being slightly giggly was jangled away with her keys.

Inside the office she sat at her desk and looked at us with her frightening cold eyes for a long time. Ordinary people would have started going on at you by now, but her way of waiting made you feel small and ashamed and wish you could evaporate. It was more effective than any kind of telling off.

'So,' she said, 'let's begin with the nuns in the attic.'

She looked at us for a moment then carried on talking quietly and calmly. 'These are stories. The reason the attic is locked is because that staircase is unsafe.

'Also, there is an old and unsafe fire escape leading from the attic to the village road. We don't want people using this fire escape to get in or out of the building. Workmen were supposed to come and replace the old fire escape over the summer but they didn't get round to it. That is why that metal gate is kept locked. Even though you shouldn't have been anywhere near it in the first place.'

'Sorry, Sister,' Bernadette said. 'It was my idea for a dare, to go into the nuns' corridor.'

'It seems to me your dare was a long way back in the events of last night. I want to move on from that and whatever cavorting madness around the bedrooms followed, and talk about Chiquita Morris.'

She looked at us as if she wanted to make sure we were listening carefully. Not that we'd have dared be doing anything else.

'Last night Chiquita tried to run away after wrecking her own room in a temper. Then she took some pliers from the tool cupboard and broke the padlock on the metal gate. She'd been hoping to climb down the fire escape from the attic but realized it was too dangerous. She was going to come out of the attic and try another way out of the building by the nun's private back door. Then she heard noises – you two scuffling about, I expect. So she stayed in the attic, waiting. It was Chiquita who had broken the padlock on the metal gate but Sister Patricia didn't know that when she called for Sister Vincent. Sister Vincent is, as you know, the PE teacher, therefore the fittest of the sisters in case it was a burglar or some other kind of intruder in the attic. Sister Patricia did not call Sister Vincent because Sister Vincent has a sister with leprosy in the attic.'

She looked at us in silence. I had a feeling she was making fun of us, just slightly.

'Do you understand what I've told you so far?'

'Yes, Sister,' Bernadette said automatically.

'Yes, Sister, but—' I said.

Sister Maria held up her hand to silence me. 'When Sister Vincent went up into the attic she found Chiquita. Chiquita was excessively upset to be caught. Screaming.

Hysterical really. That's why she is in the infirmary now, calming down. These are the straightforward explanations for last night. Do you understand what I have told you?'

We both nodded. Yes, we understood the rather boring explanation for it all.

I thought the next bit was going to be her telling us what our punishment was but Sister Maria was full of surprises.

'Bernadette,' she said, 'do you like Chiquita Morris?'

Not expecting the question, Bernadette made a vague mumbling noise.

'How about you, Katherine? I thought you were going to try to be kind to her.'

'I was,' I said. 'But she seemed to go off me.'

Again, Sister Maria looked at us till we nearly froze.

'Well, I have something more useful for you two to be doing than running about the corridors causing chaos. I want you to look after Chiquita. If you gave her a chance, you might find you liked being friends with her. What do you think, Bernadette?'

Bernadette made another mumbling sound. For Bernadette this was terrible. Her worst nightmare. To have to be friends with Chiquita Morris. Who had, after all, just said that thing about her smell, which was pretty mean.

'Perhaps it will be easier for you, Katherine, as you are new and haven't got stuck into the usual pattern of ignoring Chiquita and leaving her out of things. I'll be expecting great effort from you both.'

'Yes, Sister,' I said. Bernadette was just mumbling again.

'I don't want to hear "Yes, Sister". That isn't enough. I'll be watching to see what sort of effort you make with Chiquita. You better go to your lessons now. And remember, this is your chance to do something more important than running about scaring everyone with nonsense. This is your chance to help someone who needs help.'

When we got out into the corridor we looked at each other and made wide-eyed faces of amazement.

'That's too weird,' I said.

'Torture,' Bernadette said. 'It's a disgusting torture. How can I possibly ever be friends with her?'

'Well,' I suggested, 'we could not do it.'

'And have Sister Maria look at us?'

That's what I'd thought.

'I don't think it's possible to really be friends with her,' Bernadette said as we walked towards the classroom. 'But we could pretend to be friends to keep Sister Maria quiet and find out why Chiquita tried to run away, although it was probably nothing. Probably just Chiquita being strange for attention. This isn't the first time she's tried to run away.'

'Why did she try before?'

'I don't know. She's never had any friends. I suppose that's a reason.'

'But why? Why absolutely no friends ever?'

'I told you, she's horrible and a thief and you saw how she can be horrible yourself.'

'Is it really true she steals things? Why would she if she's rich?'

'Rich doesn't matter,' Bernadette said. 'Not if you're greedy.'

I remembered what Danielle had said about Bernadette being a suspect in those past crimes. Rich but greedy could apply to Bernadette.

Maybe Bernadette blamed Chiquita because it was really her that stole things.

Or did Danielle blame Bernadette because it was really her?

Overall, I would be happiest if the criminal was Danielle because that flicky plaited bag of smug smirkery just went from bad to worse...

I couldn't believe my ears as we went into the classroom and everyone was listening to Danielle talking about how she had stood up to Sister Ita.

'...So I said, "Sister Ita, I was simply concerned about my friend." You should have seen her silly red face! And then—'

'And then she told you to go to bed and you did, like a mouse,' Bernadette interrupted her.

'Oh, here they are,' Danielle smirked smugly. 'The dynamic duo. Or is it the terrified twins? Honestly, I'll laugh till I die when I think about you two getting the whole corridor in a panic.'

'I hope you do laugh till you die,' Bernadette said.

And whatever Danielle was going to say next was

stopped by Sister Patricia coming in. She looked tired and sort of dizzy – I suppose rushing about getting frights in your dressing gown when you're top heavy would be very dizzy making. Her veil was crooked like her head had been spun around in a spin dryer and her brown nuns' dress was hitched all wonky.

'Talk, talk, talk,' she said. 'That's the trouble with you girls. I want you all to write an essay called "Why Silence Is Golden" for your English homework tonight. You were all very silly last night so as a punishment there will no sweetshop opening for the rest of the week. Bernadette, since you're so good at getting people to do things, you will collect a pound from each girl at lunchtime and give it to me for the charity box.'

A groan went around the room.

'Quiet,' Sister Patricia said. 'No shop and a pound each in the charity box.'

The nuns had a little pretend shop beside the dining room where they sold chocolate, sweets and crisps for girls to buy with their pocket money. No sweetshop was blamed on me and Bernadette.

At the end of class, Bernadette found a jam jar in the art room to use for a collecting box. All through recreation we went around collecting the pounds, and everyone except very shy new girls complained that we'd caused this fine.

'I don't know why I listened to your stupid idea,' Bernadette said as she put the jam jar of pound coins in her desk after lunchtime recreation. 'I never got into this much trouble before, ever.'

I reminded her that she was the one who'd started the trouble with a dare.

'Don't speak to me, you're stupid and new,' she said. 'We've got netball now. Try not to be too useless.'

She stomped off to talk to Fiona and left me with no friend at all. Well, good riddance if she was going to be so moody.

I was extremely useless at netball. I was glared at by everyone, including Sister Vincent, who kept blowing on her whistle and shouting, 'Wake up, silly girl, watch the game!'

I thought it was a bit rich for a nun running around in trainers, a brown tracksuit and a veil to call anyone silly. A veil held on with a piece of white elastic under her chin. How silly was that?

When netball was, thankfully, finally over, I was one of the last back to class because I'd got my trainer laces in a knot I couldn't undo. I did that stupid thing of pulling a lace and only making the knot worse. I tried to just pull my foot out of my trainer but it was so tight and I was pulling so hard, I fell over... just as Sister Vincent came in.

'You, girl, what are you doing rolling about the locker-room floor? What kind of silliness is that?'

I explained the situation with my trainer. Sister Vincent was back in her brown nuns' dress now, although still wearing trainers and the veil with elastic. She plunged her hand into her dress pocket and pulled out a fork.

'This should do the trick,' she said, and undid the knot by poking the fork through it.

I had to ask: 'Sister Vincent, why do you have a fork in your pocket?'

'It's been useful, hasn't it? Oh yes, my dear, I've learned the kind of things children are likely to do, so I carry an array of useful implements with me at all times. Getting trapped by knots is a very common disaster among children.' She put the fork back into her pocket. It clanked against whatever other fascinating useful implements she had in there. 'Well, girl, don't stand there gawking. Put your shoes on and go back to class.'

Sister Patricia was already in the classroom as I hurried in, explaining my problem with my trainer laces.

'Never mind, never mind, sit at your desk, I don't want to hear it,' she said. Then she looked at Bernadette. 'So, Bernadette Kelly. Where is my money for the charity box?'

Bernadette opened her desk and moved the books I'd seen her put on top of the jam jar to hide it. She moved them again.

The jam jar was gone.

'It's gone!' she said in a strangled voice. 'It was right here, you saw me put it under the books, didn't you, Katherine?'

I nodded.

'Check again,' Sister Patricia said, coming towards us.

Bernadette shuffled everything out of her desk onto mine. 'Definitely gone,' she said. 'I thought it would be safe with everyone at netball.'

But not everyone had been at netball. Someone had come out of the infirmary and was now sitting at the back of the class, flicking through one of her fancy magazines as if the rest of us didn't exist. Chiquita Morris. Suspect number one.

CHAPTER FOURTEEN

Sister Patricia called Sister Maria on her mobile, saying there was a 'serious and urgent matter'. Then, with a lot of squeaking she explained about the jam jar of money being stolen.

When Sister Maria arrived, her face was like an angry icicle.

'I have to say this seems to be one of the worst Year Sevens this school has ever had,' she said quietly, but as if she'd like to pull out all our insides. 'Three days into term and there has been nothing but trouble. I shudder to think how you might continue. But I am here to tell you all that this will be the last of it. We will get to the bottom of this despicable theft of money intended for charity and there will be no more trouble from this class. Not so much as a whisper of trouble. Is that clear?'

We all nodded and I felt very sorry for whoever had stolen the money because Sister Maria would just massacre them with a single look.

Not that sorry, though. Because crime was crime, as

Grandad said, and where would we be if people all got away with crimes?

And as you can guess, I was mostly thinking it was great, perhaps now my proper boarding-school adventures would begin. The squashed-faced monster nuns in the attic might have turned out to be made-up nonsense, but here was plain old theft. A matter for what Grandad would call 'solid basic detective work'. The kind of thing that was frequently on television and couldn't go wrong in terms of having been just a matter of imagination.

First I had to look at my suspects. The main suspect was Chiquita Morris. Grandad said the most obvious person had usually not done it. Or usually had done it. You would say, 'It can't be the obvious suspect,' waste a lot of time trying less-obvious suspects and end up feeling a bit foolish back at the obvious suspect you started with.

So Chiquita Morris was suspect number one. Or not.

Grandad said you should also always look for the least-likely person. The least-likely person was Bernadette, because she was also the victim of the crime. But it wasn't her own money in the jam jar. She could just be pretending to look upset and shocked but have stolen the money herself out of sheer greed. She'd been very quick leaving the locker room after netball. Would she have had time to move the jar from under the books and hide it somewhere else? Possibly.

I tried to think of a reason why Danielle could also be a main suspect but I couldn't.

Then it occurred to me... When had Chiquita come into the classroom? Maybe she hadn't been all alone in the classroom while we'd been at netball. Maybe she came back after other people came back from netball. Other people like Bernadette, or Danielle.

I imagined myself presenting the evidence that it was Danielle in front of the whole school. Then I had to stop because I knew it was a mistake detectives often made, to want it to be the suspect they didn't like. Many famous detectives confused themselves like this. I would have to remain calm and not let personal feelings run away with me.

Sister Maria was talking about what she was going to do. We wouldn't be allowed to wear our own clothes at the weekend – people liked this chance not to wear the uncomfortable uniform, but we wouldn't be getting the chance. There would also be no television for our class on Saturday unless the money was returned. The girl who did it could come quietly to her or to Sister Patricia at any time. Or, if they were too cowardly to do that, they could anonymously return the money by Sunday night. If the girl did not own up or return the money by Sunday night, the police would be called in on Monday and the girl caught would be instantly expelled.

In the meantime, we were to continue with our lessons but Sister Ita would be searching all our gym lockers and Sister Patricia would now look in everyone's desks.

As the desk lids were opened, I couldn't see anyone who

looked nervous. But they could have put the jam jar any-where, in some secret hiding place in the garden, along the corridor…

The search of desks revealed nothing.

Sister Maria said to Sister Patricia: 'None of these girls is to go to the lavatory alone this afternoon. They must go with someone you choose. Just in case they are hiding the jar in a new place.' Then she looked at us from the doorway. 'This incident is an enormous disappointment to me.'

Not to me. To me it was proper boarding-school stuff. I'd solve the jam-jar crime and be heroic. Sister Maria would actually smile at me and Danielle would just spit with jealousy.

But in the meantime, Sister Patricia adjusted her veil and opened a book on her desk. 'The whole thing is very bad, a bad, miserable business. Now, appropriately, in history today we are going to learn about a time called the Dark Ages.'

I didn't hear anything about the Dark Ages. Or the English lesson about different kinds of punctuation. I wanted all the lessons and meals to be over so I could talk to Bernadette properly. I had decided to forgive her for being bad-tempered and going back to the old business of calling me 'new', because she was the only choice of person I had to talk to.

We had a chance to whisper on the way to the evening meal. Bernadette, less bad-tempered now, said that we could combine three jobs in one – pretend to make friends with Chiquita to keep Sister Maria quiet, pretend to make friends to find out why she tried to run off, and pretend to be friends to catch her out as the thief.

'If it's her,' I said, not sure I liked all this pretending. Part of me still felt Chiquita was a tragically sad person, thief or not.

'Everyone knows she's a thief,' Bernadette whispered, irritated I wasn't immediately agreeing with her.

'So what actual evidence of her stealing do you have?' I asked.

'I told you. Danielle invited Chiquita home at half-term a few terms ago and Chiquita stole a diamond bracelet belonging to Danielle's mum. They caught her when it fell out of her pocket at the train station. Danielle persuaded her mother not to do anything because she felt sorry for Chiquita. But she still doesn't trust her.'

I couldn't believe Bernadette hadn't thought about this before. 'But, Bernie, do you think a story from Danielle is true?'

Bernadette looked shocked and then looked awkward. 'I don't know.'

'I think Danielle's probably a liar. We need to be careful about stuff she says.'

'That's right,' Bernadette realized. 'It's all just stuff Danielle says. Not real proof.' Then she got cross. 'This doesn't mean Chiquita's a nice person.'

'Yes, yes, but we should forget about Danielle's evidence that she's a thief, it's probably just rubbish.'

'OK,' Bernadette said, looking very fed up.

I didn't tell Bernadette that Danielle also said that Bernadette was the thief. After all, Bernadette was a suspect too, so I needed to keep some secrets from her. Even if she wasn't a criminal, Bernadette obviously wasn't a very good detective if it was only just occurring to her that this 'Danielle says' business was her only evidence. So it was probably best if I kept charge of all the information for now.

Still, we had to keep near Chiquita – we might as well be sure she wasn't the criminal as well as finding out about her problems. We watched where she went after tea. As usual she wandered off to sit alone in the garden. When we caught up with her she was eating a bar of chocolate and looking at a magazine.

I'd warned Bernadette to try to be very good-tempered and patient but the first thing she said to Chiquita was: 'Hey, I thought there was no sweetshop.'

'So?' Chiquita said, showing the chocolate in her mouth. 'I have my own stores in my room. Tough for you if you don't.'

Before Bernadette could say something angry back, I asked Chiquita in a nice way, 'Are you feeling better?'

She looked at me, then looked back at her magazine.

Bernadette made an impatient sound.

I sat beside Chiquita. Niceness was what was needed, not impatient sounds. 'What are you reading?' I asked her.

'Get lost,' she said.

'Listen—' Bernadette started saying crossly.

'Yes, listen,' I interrupted. 'What do you think about this crime? Who do you suspect?' I thought this was very clever of me. It would make Chiquita think we didn't suspect her.

'I think Bernadette did it herself,' Chiquita said, without looking up from her magazine.

'Don't be so stupid! How could I?' Bernadette exploded. 'You stupid— I think it was you!'

Chiquita looked at her spitefully and said, 'You were in the classroom when I came in.'

'So were other people, so was Danielle and loads of people! Maybe you had already sneaked in while we were at netball!' Bernadette shouted. 'Sneaked in and went out again, hid the money and came back all innocent!'

Chiquita jumped up, slapped at Bernadette with her magazine, said, 'Get lost!' again and ran off.

We watched where she went. She threw herself under a tree in another part of the garden and started crying.

'It's her,' Bernadette said. 'So obvious.'

'It's never the obvious one. Except sometimes,' I said.

Bernadette looked at me as if I was talking in Martian. 'What does that mean?'

'It's a detective thing,' I said. 'My grandad is a detective.'

Bernadette looked impressed but then she got annoyed. 'I can't believe she said it was me. Did you see her? Fat greedy pig eating chocolate when she knows we've no sweetshop.'

'She's not that fat,' I said, realizing I was going to look pretty stupid if Bernadette found out my grandad only did security at Boots. But then, if she was a criminal she'd go to prison and no one would believe what she said about my grandad.

'Anyway,' Bernadette was saying, 'I think we should go and force her to confess. I can easily fight her.'

'Don't,' I said. 'I'll go and talk to her. We have to be nice to her, remember.'

'Oh, this is so stupid,' Bernadette said. 'I'm going to get Fiona and go to the den. We'll make a plan about catching Chiquita – you can talk to her and make her think we like her then we'll catch her when she doesn't expect it.'

I pretended to think Bernadette's plan was excellent. Because I had to make Bernadette think I liked her, and catch her when she didn't expect it. If she was the criminal. All this pretending – it was very brain-exhausting.

CHAPTER FIFTEEN

Where Chiquita was sitting was a beautiful spot. A patch of grass under a tree by a wall covered in old rose bushes. The last of some pink roses were bobbing around in the breeze. It was a particularly nice place to sit because you were almost hidden from the rest of the gardens; you could get some peace to think and make plans. Or cry, if you were that way inclined.

I sat down beside her. She carried on crying quietly, moving her arm across her face more, to show me she wanted me to go away.

I kept quiet for a while. What I said now would be very important. I had to think very carefully to find exactly the right thing to say …

'I can't do that,' I said.

Eventually she had to ask, 'Do what?'

'Cry if people are looking at me. I mean I used to, but now I just can't.'

Chiquita sniffed, not looking at me. 'Yeah well,' she said. 'Haven't you heard? I'm a bit stupid.'

'I haven't heard that,' I said.

Then there was a long silence. I was trying to think of another good thing to say when she suddenly looked at me angrily. 'What do you want?' She had the puffiest cried-out eyes I'd ever seen.

The truth blurted out before I could think of a good thing to say. 'I want to make friends with you,' I said.

She looked at me as if I was totally insane with no nose. She picked up her magazine and it seemed she was going to get to her feet and stomp off, but then she changed her mind.

'I thought you knew about me,' she said. There were still tears in her eyes. She looked bewildered. 'Haven't they told you I'm stupid and greedy and steal everything? And I don't even have parents.'

I didn't see what the last part had to do with anything.

'I don't have a dad, just my mum and grandad and Auntie Apricot, but she's dead now.'

Chiquita seemed even more bewildered. 'Apricot?' she said. 'You have an auntie called Apricot?'

I explained the whole thing and even imitated Auntie Apricot answering the phone sounding all posh with a cigarette in a holder.

For the first time I heard Chiquita laugh. Just a little laugh, like a snort, but it made quite a change.

'So, you're a bit of a charity case too,' she said. 'Like me.'

'Charity case? I thought you were really rich.'

She shrugged. 'Sort of. It was my dad's money. He's dead

now. He died when I was four. He didn't like my mum so he left all the money in these things called trusts for me. One of the trust things pays the nuns to look after me.' Then she looked at her hands for a moment, as if remembering watching them grow. 'I've been here since I was four,' she said sadly.

'I know,' I said. 'That must be lonely.'

'It'll be all right,' she said, shaking her black wavy hair and trying to look as though she didn't care about a thing. 'When I'm eighteen I'm going to be stinking rich. I'll travel all around the world and marry some film star and not remember anyone who's here. Bernadette, Danielle, that lot, they'll just be able to look at me in magazines and die of envy.'

'That's a long time to wait,' I said. Even if Chiquita was thirteen it would still be thousands of days at the school, lonely and crying until she was eighteen. 'Wouldn't it be better to have some friends now?'

She shook her head slowly. 'You're new,' she said. 'You don't know what they're like here. What happened to you on the first night is nothing. Wait till Danielle really gets started on you.'

'She's awful,' I said. 'I could just punch her face already.'

Chiquita looked pleased. 'I tried once but she's really strong and good at fighting. She has lots of older brothers. The only one who can really fight her is Bernadette. But Bernadette's pretty horrible too.'

'Not as bad,' I said. 'Sometimes she's funny and interesting under the horribleness.'

'Underneath,' Chiquita said thoughtfully. 'She's also completely miserable.'

'Is she?' I asked, although I thought Chiquita was probably right.

'That stuff about the operation. She won't get to leave after that. Her parents want to travel around the world without kids with them all the time. She's dumped here, like me.' Then she looked very sad. 'When I was in Junior Three here, we did lessons on the Ten Commandments. Honour your father and mother. Doesn't say anything about honouring your kids, does it?'

It was a good point. A not-very-fair thing. I told her how sometimes I felt miserable that my dad had gone off and couldn't care less about me.

'But you've got a mum.'

'Yes, and a grandad.'

'Is your mum nice?'

I didn't want to make her feel jealous but I had to say she was very nice and so was my grandad. I had to admit that now I was actually at boarding school and not dreaming about it from what I read in books, I was surprised how much I missed them already.

'But if you wrote and told them you wanted to leave, they'd let you?' Chiquita asked.

'Yes,' I said. 'But it would be a bit of a disaster, considering I just got here.'

She nodded. 'You're lucky, though,' she said. 'Being alone is just—' She stopped what she was going to say and it was as if she'd made a decision. She opened the magazine in her hand. It fell open at a page immediately. She passed it to me and pointed to a picture.

'That's my mum,' she said.

It was a page of photographs of fancy people at a fancy party.

In the largest photo there was a beautiful woman in an evening dress. There was a caption underneath it: '*In London for the royal birthday celebrations.*'

I looked at the other photos and realized some of the people were royal and the party was at a palace. I realized I knew who the woman in the photo was, even me who never read a magazine except by accident. She was Stella Diaz, one of the most famous fashion models in the world.

Then I remembered that Chiquita was supposed to be a big liar.

'If Stella Diaz is your mum...?'

She nodded sadly. 'That's why I don't tell anyone. Who would believe me?'

'No, I do believe you,' I said, even though I wasn't sure I did. 'But why do you say you have no parents? I thought both your parents must be dead.'

'That's what I thought until this holidays.' Chiquita touched the picture in the magazine with her chubby little hand. 'I was here on my own with the nuns as usual and Sister Maria took me to have my hair cut. She was trying to make me have it cut short but I argued and just had it trimmed ... Anyway, there was a long wait, so I was looking at the magazines in the hairdresser's and I saw a picture of Stella Diaz. I recognized her – I remembered my mum's name was Stella. I remembered her crying when my dad died of cancer. I remembered being brought here when I was four by my grandparents, who were always arguing with my mother. After I was here only a few days, Sister Maria told me my grandparents and my mother had been killed in a terrible car crash. I thought that was the end, all my family had been killed. But when I saw Stella Diaz in that magazine, I recognized her. Even if her surname was different, she looked exactly the same as I remembered. So Sister Maria admitted it was true, that my mother hadn't died.'

My head was spinning. Chiquita had a funny way of talking: she didn't look at you; she was all stops and starts, as if talking at all was an unusual thing for her. Perhaps it was. What a horrible thing, to be so lonely you'd nearly forgotten how to talk. I asked her if she was telling me that Sister Maria had lied to her about her mother?

'Not exactly,' Chiquita said. 'After my dad died, Stella Diaz told the family to send me to boarding school, because she wanted to be a model, and couldn't be bothered with me. She went off and left me with my grandparents. After the accident killed my grandparents, Sister Maria had written to her and begged her for years to come and take care of me, but she always said no. So Sister Maria let me go on thinking my mother was dead, rather than have false hope. When I recognized her in the magazine, I asked Sister Maria to get in touch with her again. Then Sister Maria showed me a horrible official letter from her, saying I wasn't her daughter, saying it was all lies. Sister Maria told me I should forget about Stella Diaz because she won't even admit she's my mother. But I know she's my mother.'

You could see it: you could see a little, fatter Stella Diaz in Chiquita.

'Sister Maria thinks I shouldn't read these magazines, but I have them sent to me all the time now. I never used to look at magazines. Maybe if I had, I'd have known sooner. Maybe if the nuns let us watch television more, I'd have known sooner. But now I do know and I can't forget. I like these kind of pictures best,' Chiquita said, turning a page to show more pictures of Stella Diaz at the royal party. 'Pictures where I can see what she's doing. Usually my mother's in New York, because she has a company that does make-up for women with darker skin. It's a big success and she's designing clothes now. She's originally from a country called Guatemala, in South America, that's why she looks like she does.'

Chiquita came to life as she was talking about her. It was an amazing story. Was it true?

Chiquita talked on excitedly. 'My dad was English; he met her when he was working there for a charity. He liked her in the beginning, but then he realized his family was right and she was bad, so when he died he left her nothing.

She ran off and the family brought me here, to the nuns, because they were too old to look after me on their own all the time, but I could have gone home in the holidays. But then they were killed. So there's no one. Just me and the nuns. They try to be kind. But I can't stand it now I know I shouldn't really be here.'

'No,' I said quietly, feeling a little bit like I might cry despite not being a crier. 'Who could stand it? A thing like that.'

'When I saw this picture I went crazy. I threw everything around my room and decided I was going to London. I'd find her by asking the people who worked at the palace where she was. I thought I'd just go there and make a fuss till they told me where she was staying.'

She took the magazine out of my hand, staring at the picture of her mother as if she was talking right to her.

'I thought, when she saw me, she'd be ashamed of how she acted. When she realized I'd run away to see her, she'd be sorry and everything would be different.'

'Maybe she'd be ashamed,' I said. I'd thought that exact thing about my dad, that he'd see me some time and be ashamed of what he'd done.

Chiquita shrugged and took the magazine away. 'I was crazy. Like Sister Maria told me, she'd have been gone by the time I got to London. The party in this photo was last week. It was a pathetic, stupid idea. Sister Maria says I have to think of my future and not let my mother humiliate me any more. She's a bad, careless, selfish person. She doesn't deserve me. Sister Maria says those things and gets really angry about my mother. It's kind of her. She's very kind. But I think part of me would run and jump like a hopeful dog if my mother turned up. Run and jump like a hopeful dog . . .' She paused and stared sadly into space.

'There must be some other way to get in touch with her,' I suggested.

'I did try another way – I didn't tell Sister Maria about it because she thinks I should forget about Stella – but I wrote to her make-up company in New York, because the address was in a magazine. I expect she'll just ignore it. But there's part of me that's still dreaming that maybe she won't. You don't want to be my friend, Katherine. Since I realized about my mother I'm always thinking really stupid things.'

I didn't think it was stupid. It was tragic for Chiquita, but tragic in a very glamorous way. A life so far away from my fish-fingers-for-tea-with-Grandad kind of life. It was all so beyond the normal world I was used to that I had to struggle to find any words that might help Chiquita. Nothing I knew about seemed relevant, but I tried.

'It seems to me that thinking stupid things should make us good friends,' I said. 'I'm the one who made the whole class barricade themselves in Danielle's room to escape leprosy.'

Chiquita looked at me as if I was joking. She'd missed all my drama because she'd been having her own. When I described the running and barricading to her, with actions, she started laughing and laughing. 'Stop,' she said, arms round her waist, 'you're making my stomach hurt. I can't believe you did that.'

'I know,' I said, so pleased she was laughing. 'My mum says I'm mostly fine but when I start imagining things I get carried away and turn into a crazy person.'

As the bell rang to go back to class, Chiquita and I walked back together, without even needing to say that we were definitely friends now.

'Don't tell the others,' she said as we climbed the steps into the school building. 'They'll never believe me, and if Stella Diaz never wants to see me, what proof do I have? I've still got daydreams about her, but I bet until I'm eighteen, I'm here with Sister Maria acting more like she's my mum and I'll never be normal.'

I had to agree, it was probably not normal.

CHAPTER SIXTEEN

'Did she confess? Did she tell you about why she ran away?' Bernadette whispered as I sat down next to her in the classroom for evening study.

'Not yet,' I said. 'I'm working on it.'

I thought this was a good thing to say. I didn't want to be a traitor about Chiquita to Bernadette, who might be the real criminal. Who might spitefully tell everyone about why Chiquita was carrying on in the night – it seemed to me that was a very private matter. And there was no shred of proof for Chiquita's story, except Chiquita looked like a small, round version of Stella Diaz. I could imagine a smart alec like Bernadette, or worse, Danielle, saying Chiquita had invented the whole thing after she'd noticed that she looked a bit like Stella Diaz.

And, of course, it was always possible I would look like a total idiot for believing the story enough to repeat it.

'Well, it's good you've got her confidence,' Bernadette said. 'I am going to sneak in and search her bedroom when she's getting washed tonight – you have to keep her talking in the bathroom.'

I didn't like the sound of this at all. Letting this happen would be the act of a traitor.

Sister Maria came in, glaring, so there was no more talking. We all had a lot to do. We had French and history and maths to do and we had to write our 'Silence Is Golden' essay.

'I can't believe all this homework,' I said to Chiquita on the way to our rooms. I was walking with Chiquita because I liked her. Bernadette was off ahead with Fiona and Sarah, thinking I was only talking to Chiquita as part of the traitorous plan.

Chiquita shrugged. 'I don't care about school stuff. I'm never going to get a job. I'll just go shopping and be in magazines. I never used to be interested in fashion but now I think about it all the time. I suppose it's just in my blood. What designers do you like?'

'What?' I was only half listening, wondering if it was in her blood or just in her imagination.

'Fashion designers,' she said.

I told her I didn't know because I usually got clothes off the market or from a catalogue. 'I'm not very cool like that,' I admitted.

We were interrupted because we were passing Danielle, Indira and some other fans of Danielle.

'Oh, that's a good idea,' Danielle said. 'The two weirdos together.' Her friends laughed.

I stopped and looked at her. 'Better to be weird than boring,' I said.

It wasn't a very clever thing to say but I had to say something.

As I went to catch up with Chiquita I heard Danielle doing a loud fake laugh and saying, 'See what I mean, a complete weirdo.'

Chiquita was smiling as I caught up. 'That was cool,' she said.

'Not really,' I muttered. 'She got the last laugh.'

'It's cool to try and stand up to her,' Chiquita said. 'But dangerous. Next thing you know, something stolen will turn up in your belongings.'

I looked at her, horrified.

'She's not boring,' Chiquita said. 'She's totally evil.'

CHAPTER SEVENTEEN

'Right. She's going to the bathrooms now. Keep her talking,' Bernadette said as she put on her faded dressing gown. 'Go on, quick. Get in the next bathroom and talk to her so she stays a long time.'

We were allowed three baths a week. People had to put their name on a list. Bernadette had seen Chiquita's name down for tonight and put mine down too. I tried to get out of it.

'I don't feel like a bath,' I said. 'I feel a bit sick.'

'A bath won't make you feel worse,' Bernadette said. 'Hurry up.'

'What if she won't stay talking and catches you?'

'Fiona's keeping lookout in the corridor. If Chiquita or a nun appears suddenly, I'll hide behind the curtains until the coast's clear, or she has to go to the toilet or something.'

I couldn't think how to get out of it. And yet again Bernadette had forgotten about her smell problem in the plan. She'd be sniffed out behind the curtains. But what could I say?

'Come on!' Bernadette fussed at me until I went out of the door ahead of her.

I went up the landing and glanced back to see Bernadette and Fiona talking near Chiquita's room. They were looking at me, so I carried on towards the bathrooms.

I'd quite have liked a bath really but it was more important to think of a way to avoid being a traitor to Chiquita. Suddenly, a bathroom door opened and a girl came out in a cloud of steam. Chiquita.

'What are you doing?' she asked me.

'Watching,' I told her. 'Aren't you having a bath?'

'Forgot my towel,' she said. 'What are you watching?'

I thought fast and came up with an answer I was quite pleased with. 'I want to see if anyone tries to put the jam jar in my stuff.'

Chiquita looked confused. 'What do you mean?'

'You said Danielle would put stolen things in my belongings, and the jam jar is a stolen thing.'

'Oh yes,' Chiquita said. 'Yes, that's what she's like. Like she put her mum's bracelet in my pocket that time.'

'Did she?'

'Of course.'

'But . . . even though she liked you enough to invite you to her house in the first place?'

Chiquita looked furious. 'Get lost if you don't believe me.'

'I believe you, I believe you. I just don't understand why she did it.'

Chiquita shrugged. 'I didn't understand at the time but I do now. Danielle gets jealous if anyone else gets a shred of attention from anyone. At her house her mum felt sorry for me and was really nice to me, so Danielle had to spoil it.'

'Why didn't you tell her mum the truth?'

'I was so shocked. I was just so shocked I cried and then it was too late. Danielle's mum was saying she forgave me, and it was only much later Danielle told me the truth, and told me there'd never be anything I could do about it.'

'Why didn't you tell Sister Maria or someone who likes you?'

Chiquita shrugged. 'I was scared. Danielle's a good liar. And Sister Maria seems to like her. If she turned Sister Maria against me I'd have no one at all.'

Did I believe her version of the bracelet story? I really wanted to.

'Anyway, the whole thing served me right, you know.'

'How could it?'

'When Bernadette first came here I made friends with her. We were good friends but then Danielle came and wanted to be my friend. She seemed so much more glamorous. So I dropped Bernadette. Bernadette never forgave me. When Danielle dropped me and said I was a thief, Bernadette said it served me right and she's been eternally horrible to me ever since as a punishment.'

'Bernadette never told me this.'

'She wouldn't admit she'd ever been friends with me. Not now.'

Chiquita started to go into the corridor. Fiona saw her and started coughing really loudly.

'Wait, Chiquita,' I said, 'Come back here, quick.'

If Fiona saw, she'd think I was trying to delay Chiquita, when really I was whispering to her that Bernadette would be hiding behind her curtains because she'd been searching the room.

'I'm sorry,' I said. 'I couldn't stop them.'

Chiquita didn't seem to blame me. She hurried back to her room, passing Fiona, who was coughing like crazy. I decided to go back to my room and keep out of it.

In a short while, I heard Chiquita shout something. In another while, Bernadette ran into our bedroom.

'She caught me!' she panted. 'She came in and opened the curtains. She shouted, so I ran. I didn't have a chance to search properly and I think Sister Ita's coming.'

'Oh well,' I said, getting into bed. 'I don't think it's Chiquita.' Then as I said it, I knew I was sure. 'I'm sure it's Danielle.'

Bernadette looked at me scornfully. 'You wish, you mean. I wish it was her too but wishing is just wishing.'

I told her what Chiquita had told me about the bracelet, reminding her that she'd only ever heard Danielle's version. And I told her what Chiquita had said about them being good friends once.

'That's not true,' Bernadette said. 'Chiquita's such a liar. All right, maybe when we were very little but then she got friendly with Danielle so she could go to her house and steal.'

'I don't think she did. I think Danielle tricked her into being her friend and then tricked her with the bracelet.' To convince Bernadette more, I told her what Danielle had said about Bernadette being a thief.

Maybe I should have waited with that information, as Bernadette was sort of a suspect, but hardly at all compared to Danielle. And I wanted to make sure Bernadette knew the full extent of Danielle's evil.

Bernadette shook her head, confused. 'But she ruined my friendship with Chiquita, then made everyone hate Chiquita. Danielle's always been so pretty and popular, why would she do all this?'

'Maybe so no one else can be as popular as her, even with her mum. She just plots and plans sneakily and destroys people.'

'You could be right,' Bernadette said sadly. 'Before she came here, lots of people liked me, then gradually she was the most popular, possibly by telling lots of lies about me.' She groaned and pulled her duvet up over her head. 'I hate all this. Saturday tomorrow and no own clothes, no sweet-shop, no television. I hate it here so much.'

It seemed to me, it wasn't 'here' that was the thing to hate – it was Danielle.

CHAPTER EIGHTEEN

In the morning Bernadette said she'd dreamed Danielle had put a jam jar full of bracelets in her desk – a pretty scary dream.

After breakfast, something even more scary than bracelet dreams happened to Bernadette. She was called into Sister Maria's office. And quite quickly came out again, looking worried.

'She wants to see you next,' she said. 'She's asking about Chiquita: she says she doesn't believe we're trying to be friends.'

'But we are,' I said indignantly.

'That's what I said, but she doesn't believe me. Says she saw Chiquita hitting me with a magazine and running away crying. She's completely spying on us, it's disgusting. You better hurry and go to her office. She's in a really bad mood.'

Sister Maria was behind her desk. 'I expect the other one has told you that I'm very dissatisfied,' she said. 'I asked you to be kind to Chiquita and I see little evidence of it.'

'I think I have been kind,' I said, not too loudly in case it sounded like arguing.

'Really?' Sister Maria raised one eyebrow.

'Bernadette doesn't know because I didn't think it was right to tell anyone else, but I don't think Chiquita would have told me about her mother if she didn't feel I was a real friend.' As I started to talk about the picture in the magazine, Sister Maria held her hand up and stopped me.

'That's all right, Katherine. I believe you have genuinely made an effort with Chiquita. Obviously she's confided her secret in you. And you must guard that secret carefully. It's all a very sad business.'

'So it's true?' I blurted out.

'No,' Sister Maria said sadly. 'Poor Chiquita thinks it is and I can't convince her otherwise. I don't know what to do, really, except hope that she forgets about the whole fantasy soon. Did you tell her you believed her, Katherine?'

'Mostly I did believe her, Sister.'

'That's good. I was worried that if she told the wrong girls she'd just be mocked and ridiculed. I need you to try to get her interested in other things, stop her living in this lonely fantasy she's created, or who knows where it might lead. But don't tell her you know it's a fantasy. Remember, it's a terrible thing to have no family at all. She must be handled kindly. Can you be kind and keep quiet about the truth for her, Katherine?'

I was ready to fall over with shock. Sister Maria was suddenly talking to me as if I was a person she liked. She was talking as if we were equals. I could see a new, non-scary Sister Maria now. The Sister Maria who was kind to Chiquita.

'I'll just act like I believe her.'

'Good. She's a fragile child, close to breaking point as it is. Perhaps if she's going to try anything like running away again, you can talk her out of it. Or at least get help before there's some sort of accident.' Then she looked at me sharply. 'And you're to tell no one. None of the other girls. None.'

I nodded. 'Of course I won't,' I said.

I waited while Sister Maria gave me one of her long, cold stares. I thought she might be deciding whether to trust me with her next plan about Chiquita. But no. The liking me and treating me as an equal was over now.

'Just as a matter of interest, Katherine, what do you think about this stealing?'

I could tell her about Danielle. Surely Sister Maria must like Chiquita more than Danielle – she was practically acting as a mum to Chiquita. Surely she would believe that Danielle should be suspect number one in this case, and she'd get on with sorting things out in an elegant, scary although obviously secretly kind-hearted way.

But what if Chiquita was right and even mind-reading Sister Maria couldn't see through Danielle? Also, I'd never seen a detective on television tell their teacher to solve the problem for them.

'It's a shock,' was all I said for the time being.

'It's not the kind of thing we expect in a school like this,' Sister Maria said, looking me right in the eye. 'Whatever goes on at other schools.'

I realized she was looking me in the eye like that because I was her number-one suspect. Me with my 'underprivileged background'.

If only I'd told her about Danielle, but it was too late now. It would look like I was quickly trying to blame someone else.

'I hope it's sorted soon, Sister,' I mumbled.

'Oh, it will be, Katherine, it will be,' she said, opening a book on her desk. It seemed she'd finished with me.

I nodded and got out of there quickly. I realized I was shaking a bit. Not from fear, from anger. Furious that I was being suspected now and that Danielle was getting away with being the biggest thief and cow on earth.

It was Saturday morning and if the criminal hadn't owned up by Sunday night the police could turn up and solve everything. Or pin the blame on the wrong person. If I didn't think very hard and quickly how to solve the crime, me or Chiquita or Bernadette could be wrongly accused and put in jail.

CHAPTER NINETEEN

Everyone was out in the gardens. Everyone except our class was in their own clothes.

Most of the older girls were very fashionable, dancing around radios, or putting make-up on each other. It reminded me of my old school, where there was always a sort of competition going on about clothes. Unless you were like me, and just liked wearing jeans and T-shirts. I was scruffy more by choice than really being poor.

Even though Sister Maria might have decided I was suspicious and 'underprivileged', I wasn't one of the poor kids at my old school, not by a long way. There were kids there whose parents had no jobs; refugee kids; kids in care homes... I was actually sort of middling about money matters. But even the richest kid in that school, Louis Branco, whose dad owned the huge ice-cream place in Burnt Oak, only had a big house and some holidays in Italy. I suspected that kind of richness was nothing compared to people like Chiquita, Bernadette or Danielle. Especially Danielle.

Chiquita said Danielle's family had a sort of stately home surrounded by fields full of horses and deer. And inside the massive stately home there were huge wooden tables, marble staircases and suits of armour. On the walls were valuable paintings, tapestries and stuffed deer's heads just hanging there.

I realized that in this school there were people so rich they probably didn't even know there were people like my mum who had to work late in hospitals, or refugees, or kids in care homes because all their family were in jail or taking drugs. And yet, these unbelievably rich, deer's-heads-on-the-wall people were fighting and crying, making up massive lies and stealing. Grandad said that boarding school could show me a whole world I'd never imagined. He was so right. I'd never imagined rich people would be such a mess.

Anyway, where were we...? It was Saturday morning now – time was ticking by, as they always said on crime programmes. And the more time passes the more likely the crooks are to get away with it.

Bernadette came rushing up to me on the garden steps. She wanted to know why I'd been with Sister Maria for so long. I lied and said I'd been to the toilet – lavatory – on the way out to the garden.

'Well, hurry up now. We're all going to the den to make a plan.'

In the den, Fiona and Sarah were already waiting, and Bernadette said, 'Remember, anything said in this den is a secret on pain of being thrown to Sister Benedict with leprosy.'

'Is that true?' Sarah asked. 'I mean, I thought all that stuff in the attic was just Chiquita Morris?'

'Shut up,' Bernadette said. 'You're just a new girl, you don't know what other terrible things there really are here. We've no time for interruptions. There's already no sweet-shop, no telly or own clothes and who knows what might happen next week, because some greedy thief won't give back twenty-one pounds.'

'It's not twenty-one,' Sarah said nervously, and Bernadette looked like she might hit her.

'That's right,' Fiona chipped in. 'It's twenty pounds because Chiquita was in the infirmary.'

Suddenly a big burst of joy flooded though me. 'That's right,' I yelped. 'Chiquita wasn't there, she didn't know the money had been collected. She didn't know it existed. She couldn't possibly be the thief!'

The others muttered things like 'That's true' and 'Good point'.

Bernadette looked livid she hadn't thought of it. Then she had to give in. 'That's right, I'd forgotten that. Chiquita wasn't included. It was only twenty pounds.'

'We should get Chiquita and let her be in the den gang,' I said.

'Whatever for?' Bernadette said. 'OK, in this case she's obviously innocent because she didn't even know I had to collect money but she can't come in the den.'

'It would be friendly,' I said, looking at Bernadette with my eyes wide to show her that I meant more than I was saying.

'Oh,' Bernadette said, remembering we were supposed to be friendly to Chiquita. 'Well all right, in future she can join in but don't go getting her specially.'

'What if she's sitting somewhere all lonely, and Sister Maria sees her?'

'Oh, all right.' Bernadette said crossly. 'Go and look for stupid Chiquita.'

'What's Sister Maria got to do with it?' Fiona wanted to know.

'Nothing,' Bernadette said even more crossly. 'Katherine is just weird. Go on then, Katherine, if you're going. We have to hurry up and make a plan.'

I stomped off, annoyed with her bossiness and the way she endlessly insisted on calling me Katherine instead of Katie.

Chiquita was in her own den, under the tree by the wall and the roses. She looked guilty when I turned up because she was eating chocolate in the really very greedy, messy way she ate.

'It's just me,' I said.

She looked at me and offered me some chocolate.

I sat with her, eating chocolate. Me eating in what I hope was a less showing-everything-practically-down-to-the-insides-of my-stomach type of way.

I told her what we'd all realized in our den – that she

hadn't even known there was money to steal. So actually she was the least-suspected person in the whole school.

Chiquita said nothing, just finished eating her chocolate.

'So now you have to help us find the real person.'

'Why?' she asked. 'Who cares?'

Chiquita was peculiar beyond peculiar.

'What if it's Danielle?' I said, to tempt her.

'That would be nice. But look, I'm still really fed up, so the idea of being in some kind of tree house with Bernadette and her wee smell is really not great for me.'

'Don't be like that,' I said. 'She has a disease.'

'I know, I know, so no one can say anything to her. But she can say what she likes.'

This was a good point. I bet if Bernadette had been eternally punishing Chiquita she must have said some pretty awful things over the years.

I could have left Chiquita in peace but I felt as if she'd just rot there under the tree with her magazines, daydreaming about people who looked a bit like her and imagining they were her mother. Daydreaming about years from now when she'd be rich and in magazines herself. In between that time she was going to waste a lot of her life if I didn't think of something to cheer her up and stop her needing to make up celebrity mothers. A real mother, even a borrowed one, might help.

'You know it would be really nice if you'd come to my house in London for the holidays. It's only a small house but we could have a laugh.'

'Where in London?' she asked me, looking very surprised.

'Sort of Burnt Oak and Colindale, halfway between. We can go on the tube to the centre really easily.'

Chiquita's eyes filled with tears. I knew some people thought my part of London was a dump but I didn't see why she had to cry about it.

'What's wrong?' I asked, then I realized she was crying but smiling too. Very weird.

'You don't know me,' she said.

'Well, by the holidays we'll know each other really well, it's ages away. Why are you crying?'

'I'm just surprised,' Chiquita sniffed. 'It's a big surprise.'

'You cry when you're surprised?'

'I cry about everything.' She smiled wide, still crying.

'And my mum doesn't have any jewels so I won't do any tricks on you.'

She looked at me as if she thought I was serious.

'I'm joking,' I said. 'My mum's just nice and funny, although she swears a lot when she's annoyed but we just ignore that. Anyway, come on, let's see what Bernadette's doing. Maybe it's interesting.'

Chiquita wiped her nose with her hanky and sniffed hard. 'I doubt it,' she said. 'I'll see you later. I want to finish reading this anyway.' She picked up a magazine that seemed to be all shiny pictures. 'But thanks. Thanks for the holiday thing. That's nice.'

I went off wondering what I'd let myself in for. If she did

all that crying around Grandad she'd drive him demented. But perhaps it would be all right if I explained about her weird life. If I could get her a bit more interested in crimes then she'd probably get on fine with Grandad. Mum wasn't a problem – she'd feel sorry for her fairly quickly, because that's what Mum was like.

Bernadette didn't seem to be doing anything useful in the den. She'd thought of secretly following Danielle around to see what she did. So all they'd been doing was darting about the trees, practising secret following skills.

'Tailing,' I said. 'In proper crimes it's called tailing. It takes a lot of practice: we don't have time.' And I didn't like to say, but it would be very difficult for Bernadette to be secretly following anyone.

'What do you suggest then?' Bernadette asked sulkily.

'I think we should do what you did with Chiquita. Sneak up and search her room.'

'We're not allowed upstairs now,' Bernadette said.

'That's why we'll have to sneak.'

We agreed it was good plan. Fiona and Bernadette would search. Me and Sarah would keep watch. If we saw a nun coming near the bedroom stairs I could pretend to fall over.

'Why would you fall over just like that?' Bernadette looked confused.

'Look.' I showed her. 'I suddenly start walking and then pretend I've tripped.'

Bernadette thought it was very funny. I was pleased. It

was a good trick of mine and one of the few things in life I could afford to be big-headed about.

But a bell rang before I had a chance to do it for real. Sister Ita was ringing the bell and calling all our form to go to the classroom.

Obviously it was about the crime. Had someone been caught? Had someone owned up? Had Danielle planted the evidence on someone? On me?

CHAPTER TWENTY

We took our seats in the classroom, all muttering about
how it must be about the crime. Except Chiquita, of course:
she was looking at a magazine.

Sister Patricia came in first, and we stood up.

'Good afternoon, Sister Patricia.'

She nodded and Sister Maria followed her in, looking
calm but cold.

'Good afternoon, Sister Maria.'

'Sit down,' she said.

Then she waited – long after we'd all settled, she waited.
Looking at us as if she was thinking whether we should all
be hanged, or maybe just some of us and she couldn't quite
decide.

Even Sister Patricia got nervous and let out a squeak
that she pretended was a cough, making her whole bosom
shake.

Finally, Sister Maria said: 'The distressing matter of the
theft has been resolved. The jar of money was left by my
door this morning. I take it that the girl does not wish to

own up. Well, perhaps we have no desire to know what kind of girl would do such a thing. But, I warn you that if there is ever so much as the theft of a pencil again, I will not rest until the culprit is exposed, expelled and disgraced for the rest of her life. So this girl has got off lightly on this occasion – except she should remember what she did when she goes to confession next Friday. And she should remember that she has to show the Lord himself that she repents of her time as a thief. Only then will she be truly forgiven.' With that Sister Maria swooped out like the most terrifying cleaving angel ever created.

Sister Patricia squeaked and said, 'Quickly now, Form One, change into your own clothes. Sister Vincent will take you out on a walk and maybe we'll see about television later.' She scooted out, little legs scrabbling to catch up with Sister Maria's majestic strides.

'Phew,' someone said.

'I hate walks,' Bernadette said.

Then everyone started saying about how scary Sister Maria was and how glad they were it was over. Except Danielle, who suddenly marched up to the front of the class, clapped her hands for attention and said, 'I just want to say that I for one am not satisfied with that. I still intend to find out who the thief is and expose them because I can't rest easy in a class where a thief sits laughing at me.'

Most people just stared.

'Don't be such a show-off,' Bernadette said. 'What do you know about catching thieves anyway?'

'You'll see, Bernadette Kelly,' Danielle said, tossing back her blonde plait. 'I already have a good deal of evidence.'

She marched out of the classroom, I think trying to walk like Sister Maria.

'She's totally mad,' Bernadette said.

'I think she's right,' Indira the princess said. 'I think Sister Maria has been naive and lenient.'

'What's that, big-words disease?' Bernadette said, which I thought was quite funny.

Indira glared at her and went after Danielle.

'Trouble is,' said Bernadette as we went upstairs to change, 'I'll always wonder who it was too.'

'I agree,' I said. 'Perhaps the thief will strike again, but in the meantime we should find a new crime to be getting on with. A really exciting one. You know, like the nuns in the attic – only true.'

Bernadette glared at me. 'Maybe I know lots that are completely true,' she said. 'But I'll have to decide if I want to tell a new girl.'

Bernadette was very irritating and I was sorry I'd begun to think she was interesting and funny. Probably that had been a huge mistake. 'How long before I'm not new?' I asked her.

'Oh,' Bernadette said as she banged open the wardrobe, 'you're such a big-head. It's disgusting. New girls are always big-headed and nothing but trouble. You're new till the end of this term but I'm stuck with you for now and that's that.'

CHAPTER TWENTY-ONE

As we were going up hills where it could get cold very suddenly, we had to take jumpers on the walk. Sister Vincent looked extra mad in big brown hiking boots with a red jumper tied around the middle of her nuns' outfit.

We had to walk in twos – a crocodile, it was called – winding along the side of the country roads.

I apologized to Bernadette for saying the nuns weren't true but she was still more or less ignoring me, even though she had to walk with me. Chiquita was walking at the back and seemed to be in some kind of bad mood with me as well. I told Bernadette we should walk at the back to be near Chiquita. She didn't want to but I persuaded her it was to look friendly to Chiquita in front of the nuns, but really I was hoping to find out what on earth was wrong now.

Chiquita didn't speak when I asked if she was pleased the crime was solved, or answer when I asked her what she thought would be on television. She just looked at the ground and kept walking.

Fiona and Sarah walked in front of us. This kept

Bernadette happy. Bernadette talked to Fiona about how much they hated walks.

I quite liked the walk, although there was nothing to see but green countryside and little falling-down stone walls with sheep behind them. Occasionally there was a farmhouse, even one with a thatched roof and chickens in the garden, like a perfect postcard picture of a farmhouse.

Sister Vincent was at the front to tell the girls which way to go. After a while, she panted back towards us and said: 'You, Bernadette. Your job is to keep this back section moving – I don't want any stragglers.' And she galloped off to the front again.

'She's so stupid,' Bernadette said. 'All the girls at the back could be attacked by a murderer with an axe and she wouldn't realize.'

'Or we could run away,' I suggested. 'Jump over a wall and be gone for days.'

Bernadette looked interested. 'Where would we go?'

'I don't know. Just keep going until we found the hideout of a criminal gang, got kidnapped but eventually overpowered them and got them arrested.'

'That would be interesting,' Bernadette admitted. 'But I wouldn't like to be out on these moors at night. Supposedly they're full of maniacs and gigantic dogs.'

'And it would be cold.' Fiona shivered as she put on her jumper. 'If it's this cold in the middle of the afternoon imagine how cold it would be at night.'

It was getting much colder. Up ahead I could see Sister

Vincent had put on her red jumper. It was vast, almost down to her knees. Any longer and she'd have looked like a nun trying to disguise herself as Father Christmas.

As I put on my jumper I noticed there was mist now, swirling towards us. Swirling fast. The sky seemed to be getting darker.

'Look at the mist,' I said to Chiquita, trying to draw her into the conversation. 'Amazing, like in a horror film.'

Chiquita acted as if she hadn't heard me. Just kept walking with her head down and a fed-up expression on her face. I couldn't think what I'd done to cause this.

'It's not really mist,' Bernadette said. 'We're going so high we're inside a cloud. You wait, if we go much further it'll get really horrible.'

It wasn't horrible, it was great. You could hardly see the person in front of you.

Suddenly we heard Sister Vincent shouting something. Then we bumped into Sarah, who had just bumped into the person in front of her, who had just bumped into—

'Sister Vincent says stop!' someone up ahead shouted.

We all stopped in a bit of a heap. Sister Vincent appeared beside us, dialling on a mobile phone.

'You children at the back may not have heard me. We're going to go back to that picnic area we passed and wait for Sister Ita to come with some tea and biscuits in the car. Don't want my walkers getting downhearted. Come on, Chiquita, you and I to the fore.' She took Chiquita by the hand and talked on her phone. 'Ita? Yes, wretched cloud's come down, better have tea early, no point going further. Up on the Warwick Moor road, about half a mile on from the thatched cottage. Tremendous, Ita, we'll see you soon.' She clicked off her phone and put it in her pocket. Then she rummaged in her other pocket. 'Aha!' she said, and brought out a little torch. 'Trusty flashlight! Keep your eyes on the beam, girls!'

The torch glowed a bit but there was hardly any light. Sister Vincent tutted and put it back in her pocket. 'Ignore flashlight instructions, girls! Bit of a battery crisis. Never mind! Step up, you girls, and keep close together, tea's on its way.' Then she bellowed out to the mist-hidden girls in the distance. 'We're turning back! Hold the hand of the girl in front of you. Pass it along, don't want any stragglers!'

As we walked, we all got giggly, trying walk forwards, holding hands with people behind. Sister Vincent had Chiquita by one hand and Bernadette by the other. I had Bernadette by one hand, Fiona by the other...

'Keep up! Keep up!' Sister Vincent kept roaring, pulling Bernadette along.

I was pulling Fiona, who was pulling Sarah... A very strange way of going along the road but it kept us together.

'We should be about there now!' Sister Vincent bellowed. 'Turn off the road now! Pass it back!'

There were shouts to turn off back along the line. Some cheeky person imitated Sister Vincent's deep voice.

As we went off the road there was a moment's patch of

clear air and we could see wooden picnic tables and benches.

'Gather around the central table!' Sister Vincent seemed to be quite enjoying herself, with plenty of excuses to shout loudly.

Then, as quickly as it had cleared, the mist, or cloud, was thick again. I could hardly make out Bernadette's face beside me.

'Gather around, gather around!' Sister Vincent was bellowing. 'Now, provisions are on the way, so find yourself a place to rest, but don't wander off. By the saints above I implore you not to wander off!'

Everyone shuffled around finding good places to sit.

I whispered to Bernadette, 'Let's sit with Chiquita, I need to find out why she's ignoring me.'

Before Bernadette could moan or say anything, Sister Vincent was roaring again. 'What about a sing-song, girls? Keep ourselves cheery. Any suggestions? What about "Ten Green Bottles"?' Then Sister Vincent started singing, like a huge lion was having its stomach trodden on by elephants. *'Ten green bottles…'*

Everyone started to join in, including Bernadette, obviously glad of the excuse not to hear me talking about Chiquita.

I crept around to see where Chiquita was. She had been somewhere beside Sister Vincent. I crept with the sound of Sister Vincent's lion in pain to guide me.

'Ow!' someone said when I trod on them. Not Chiquita, Indira. Indira glaring at me. I kept going. It was difficult because you could only see who people were by going right up to them.

The singing got louder and I realized it was hopeless. I sang a bit myself. We were down to one green bottle now.

Then for a few seconds the mist cleared and I saw I was facing in the opposite direction to everyone else, and I just caught a glimpse of Chiquita. Leaving through the trees.

CHAPTER TWENTY-TWO

I started after Chiquita and then the mist came down again. I started to run, fell over a tree stump or something and yelped in fright, thinking of maniacs with axes. All this happened just at the moment the song stopped, so Sister Vincent heard me yelp.

'What's that? Is someone hurt?'

'No, Sister, I tripped.'

'Who is that?'

'Katherine Milne,' I said, moving back towards them. I had hurt my knee a bit but it didn't seem too serious. 'I need to find my friend Bernadette.'

'Bernadette, call out!' Sister Vincent ordered.

'I'm here!' she shouted.

'Keep calling, Bernadette, so she can follow your voice. Tripped-over girl, are you all right?'

'Yes, Sister.'

'Tripped-over girl, are you sure you don't feel dizzy or weak in the limbs?'

'No, Sister.'

'Move slowly, in case you're hurt in some way. Where's your friend? Why isn't she calling out?'

'Over here! I'm over here!' Bernadette shouted.

'That's it, keep calling.'

Bernadette shouted really loudly, 'Over here!' and it was almost in my face.

'I found her!' I shouted.

'Splendid. Well done, tripped-over girl!' Sister Vincent shouted. 'Now, in honour of the tripped-over girl, how about "London Bridge Is Falling Down"?'

They all started singing, except me. I pulled Bernadette's arm to make her stop and listen to me.

'Chiquita's run away,' I whispered.

'What?'

'I just saw her when the mist cleared. She's run away.'

'Tell Sister Vincent.'

'No.' I decided this about the same time I said it. 'They'll just bring her back and she'll run away again and it'll go on and on. But if we find her, she'll be sure we're her friends and maybe then she'll be happy and stop running away.'

'I'm not her friend,' Bernadette said crossly.

'Come on. Please.' To be honest, I was a bit scared to go off adventuring in the mist all on my own. Chiquita might be brave out there without a friend but I wasn't. So even a not-very-good friend like Bernadette would have to do.

'Come on, before she gets too far away.'

'We'll get in such trouble.'

'Not if we rescue her,' I said. 'Not if we properly make

friends and bring her back. It'll really show Sister Maria we're her real friends. Please.'

I started moving. I knew I'd have to go with or without Bernadette, scared or not. For one thing, I realized I'd been talking about running away earlier on the walk. I could have put the idea back in Chiquita's head and if she was eaten by wild dogs or killed by maniacs it would be my fault. And another thing, it was just too sad that she was out there on her own, running away to a fantasy.

'OK,' Bernadette said. 'But once we've rescued her that better be the end of having to be friends with her.'

Just as the group started singing 'Frère Jacques', we crept away into the dark depths of the mist.

It was hard to creep carefully and go fast enough. We needed to go far enough to be out of sight in case there was another gap in the mist. Maybe Sister Vincent, or a snitch like Danielle, could spot us during a clear patch if we didn't hurry far enough away. We gripped onto each other and kept stumbling.

'This is stupid. We'll break our necks. And we don't know which way Chiquita went,' Bernadette said, which was probably true.

The mist was making all my clothes damp. This wasn't helping how cold I felt. My face and hands in particular were freezing. I expected, what with being so skinny, Bernadette was even colder than I was.

After another ten minutes of tripping up and creeping along we couldn't hear the singing. This meant there was no turning back. We'd never have found the others again without being able to hear them.

Now, I expect you're not supposed to do this – to say about things going on that you didn't know were going on at the time – but I think it's important for you to know the thing going on at the time that I didn't know was going on at the time. The thing I know now, obviously. Oh well, this is my story of crimes, nuns and things going on, so I expect I'm allowed to tell it in the order I want. I don't think there are police about such things.

What I didn't know was, meanwhile, in the nuns' yellow car, Sister Patricia was quite close to Sister Vincent and the girls in the picnic area. She'd already set out on an emergency mission just before Sister Vincent called Sister Ita about tea and biscuits. Sister Ita would go looking for the yellow car and be told Sister Patricia had gone off in it and be told why. Sister Patricia was looking for Bernadette.

Bernadette had to go to hospital immediately. They had a cancellation and the surgeon that could do her operation was available first thing Monday. She had to be in hospital getting ready that night or miss the chance and have to wait another month. Her parents had been phoned urgently in Hong Kong but no one had tracked them down yet, but never mind... Bernadette was going to be saved from wee smells and possibly getting very sick when she was older.

Except she was out in the cold mist, lost on her adventure with me.

So meanwhile, Sister Patricia raced to the picnic site and

Sister Ita, who hadn't been able to find the yellow car, had found out about the emergency and phoned Sister Vincent back. Sister Vincent had started asking for Bernadette and was panicking that she seemed to be missing.

When Sister Patricia arrived, all flustered from driving, because it's not easy to drive when you have enormous bosoms and short arms and legs, Sister Vincent was in a huge fluster herself, having lost Bernadette. And lost me, but no one was very interested in me. And because no one ever noticed her anyway, no one had even realized yet that Chiquita was missing too.

As the mist was bad and in a few hours it would be night, Sister Patricia and Sister Vincent decided the best thing was to call the police.

Meanwhile...

Me and Bernadette were stumbling along and arguing a bit because we were freezing cold and getting hungry. I was beginning to think that as adventures went, this wasn't a very good one. Bernadette wasn't helping, continually listing all the things she could think of to frighten us: 'It's so dangerous out here – wild dogs, old mine shafts, escaped convicts – and we could be lost for days, starving and freezing until nothing remains but our dead bodies, or ...'

We saw a light ahead of us. Fuzzy in the mist, but definitely the light of a house.

'Imagine living out here,' I said. 'Still, we can ask them for food and if they've seen Chiquita.'

'Don't be stupid,' Bernadette said. 'They could be

anybody. It could be a disused place with some maniacs hiding out in it. Or they could be just normal farmers who'll phone the nuns.'

'We'll look in the windows,' I said. 'See what we think of them. Maybe if they go to bed we can sneak in and steal some food.'

'No, we can't,' Bernadette said. 'That's disgusting.'

'It's all right to steal from them if they're criminals,' I told her, but she wasn't convinced.

She did agree that we should sneak up and look in the windows – in case Chiquita was tied to a chair and being held at gun point. Or in case she was in there having a lovely meal and had made friends with the people.

'If the people are nice, maybe they can give us all a lift to London,' I said. Because suddenly I just wanted to go home.

'A lift to London?' Bernadette sounded like I'd said we could get a lift to a rat-infested sewer.

'It's where Chiquita will be trying to go,' I said. 'And when we see my grandad, he'll know what to do about Chiquita.'

Then I wanted to tell Bernadette about Chiquita and her imaginary supermodel mum in the magazines. It was such a sad story. Surely no one would use it to laugh at poor Chiquita. It would help Bernadette see why we had to rescue her. But if she was still going to eternally punish Chiquita for breaking off their friendship...So I just told Bernadette that my grandad was very wise and my mum was very kind – so going there seemed the best plan.

I expected Bernadette to argue. To say that London was common and disgusting – something like that. But she surprised me. She just asked quietly, her words melting into the mist: 'And they'll be pleased to see you if you suddenly turn up?'

'I expect they'll make some fuss,' I said. 'But they'll be pleased to see me in the end.'

'You're lucky,' Bernadette said after a while. 'Imagine if you couldn't ever leave. Imagine being left at school for ever, all your stuff getting old, year after year at school.'

Bernadette had a catch in her voce. She was crying. Stumbling through the middle of nowhere, crying over Chiquita Morris, the girl she said was so disgusting. Then I realized it wasn't Chiquita. Bernadette was crying over herself. She had the stuff getting old, year after year at school.

'You're not her,' I said, and stopped walking. I put my arm round her skinny shoulders and could feel them shaking with sobs. 'Your parents see you whenever they can, even though they live in such a faraway place. You have your little brothers. You have all those brothers who love you, and your mum visiting for luxurious times in hotels and buying you a bike.'

She sniffed and nodded. 'You're right,' she said. 'It's not the same as her. It's not so bad, not nearly so bad. It's just they won't let me leave. They'd never be all right about it if I ran away – I know they'd just send me back.'

I expect being cold and hungry on the creepy moors was making her less the usual stroppy Bernadette. The only thing I could think of was to tell her that if she ran all the way to Hong Kong, her parents would be pretty impressed and let her do what she liked.

She laughed a bit and sniffed hard to finish crying. 'I suppose,' she said.

'And, anyway, you're good at everything at school, you have friends.'

'Not many.'

'Fiona's your friend.'

'Sort of. Just because no one else noticed her. But now I bet she prefers Sarah. They go well together, both sort of nice but not interesting.'

'Maybe,' I said. Although I remembered the Chinese-burn introduction, so I didn't think Fiona was that nice.

'Anyway,' Bernadette was saying, 'whenever I have a friend a new girl always comes and takes them away. People act like they're my friend but as soon as they get the choice...'

So this was why Bernadette hated new girls so much: they could be friend-stealers.

'Not all new girls are like Danielle was,' I pointed out.

Bernadette looked cross. 'Mostly they are. Who cares? I'm top at everything so I'm too busy for silly friends.'

I wanted to say that despite her bossiness and bad-temperedness I didn't mind being her friend, but was scared she'd give me a mean answer and make me have to push her in the mud or something. So I just said, 'Anyway, I'm in the same boat. Except I'm not top at anything.'

Bernadette laughed. 'Except showing off.' Then she smiled in an almost truly friendly way. 'But it sounds pretty nice at your house. Let's find Chiquita and go there even if we don't get a lift.'

I said we would. But first we had to check out the farmhouse.

As we crept closer to the house it seemed scarier.

'You know,' Bernadette whispered, 'I'm not sure this looks like a house for normal farmers.'

'Shh,' I said, in case she started some kind of no-nose leprous beast kind of story and freaked me out.

It was a very old house, like a witch's cottage. Unfortunately it wasn't made of sweets and gingerbread, just lumpy stones. There were no curtains on the windows, which made me think we were more likely to find criminals than normal farmers. I noticed the light bulb had no shade. Normal farmers would have a lampshade, surely.

As I was slightly taller than Bernadette I could see in the window best. We crouched low till we were alongside it, then flattened ourselves against the wall.

I was terrified that the minute I peeped my head forwards to see what was inside, any people in there might immediately blow my head off with a gun.

'Go on,' Bernadette whispered. 'Take a look.'

I leaned my head forwards a tiny inch. Nobody shot me.

I couldn't see any furniture. The room was as bare as the

light bulb that lit it. There was a piece of rolled-up carpet and a broom leaning against the wall beside a pile of rubbish. There were some shadows. People.

Leaning forwards a tiny inch more I heard a woman's voice.

'No. I'm telling you you're wrong, completely mistaken. Wrong.'

I thought I knew the voice. The woman was talking to a man in a grey suit. She was pacing to and fro, so I had to wait till she walked into my line of vision. Then I nearly shrieked with fright worse than if she had blown my head off with a gun. There, in a plain dark blue suit, with no veil on, was Sister Maria.

As well as the non-nun outfit, she didn't look like herself in many other ways. She was really angry. I'd been confused by her voice because I'd recognized it – but I hadn't recognized it on the verge of shouting. Her calm face was twisted and almost ugly, she was so furious.

I realized she wasn't talking to the man. There was someone else in the room I couldn't see.

Bernadette was making faces at me, wanting to know what was happening, but I had no time to talk to her now.

I ducked down to get to the other side of the window and saw that Sister Maria was talking so angrily to a fantastically glamorous-looking woman. She was talking to Stella Diaz.

CHAPTER
TWENTY-THREE

Bernadette was too curious to wait for me to tell her what was happening. She started to cross to the other side of the window – but stood on something that made her twist her ankle. She squealed in pain. Stella Diaz and the man looked at the window, and I could hear Sister Maria say, 'What was that?'

I grabbed Bernadette, who was wincing and rubbing her ankle. I pulled her over to my side of the window and then round to the side of the house.

'We'll have to run,' I said.

At the front of the house a very fancy car was parked beside the nuns' best car – a black one they used for serious occasions. A man in a chauffeur's uniform was standing beside the fancy car, smoking.

The front door opened and Sister Maria came out.

'Did you see anyone around here?' she asked him.

He threw down his cigarette and said he hadn't.

'Probably just some animal,' Sister Maria said, and went back into the house.

What Sister Maria said seemed to make the chauffeur nervous. He got in the car and shut the door. He rolled up the window so it was only open a tiny inch. Then he turned the radio on to keep himself company.

Meanwhile Bernadette was making frantic faces, and mouthing, 'Sister Maria?'

We had to get away from the house. If Sister Maria caught us when she was this angry... We had to get away to be safe – and we had to get away so I could explain to Bernadette that what I'd seen was even more strange than seeing Sister Maria.

It was almost dark now and still very misty. Behind the cars was a small road that led from the house. If we could creep past and get on that road, it would be better than stumbling around in wild fields and falling down a mine shaft.

I pointed to the road. Bernadette nodded, her face showing she was still in pain but she'd manage.

We went slowly, keeping away from the cars. With any luck the chauffeur wouldn't hear us over the radio anyway. We didn't make any noise at all but, by huge bad luck, just where we had to pass the empty nuns' car there was a small building like a garage sticking out. There was hardly any space between it and the car. As I squeezed past, the car's very loud alarm went off.

I grabbed Bernadette and we ran down the road. There was a wall down either side. No way off the road. They'd find us for sure.

We ran, getting out of breath, Bernadette making little winces of pain. Finally I saw a gap in the wall. I pulled Bernadette through it. We fell down behind the wall and lay there. Panting. Listening to the car alarm.

The car alarm stopped. I could hear Sister Maria's voice. Then it must have been the chauffeur talking. 'A couple of kids,' he said. 'Went down that way.'

CHAPTER TWENTY-FOUR

Considering she'd run on an ankle that hurt like torture, I thought Bernadette was brave to whisper: 'Shall we keep going along here behind the wall?'

I didn't think so. It didn't sound like they were chasing after us or anything. Perhaps they'd decided we were just some kids who lived out on the moors, whatever kind of kids those were.

I knew what Bernadette's next question would be: 'And what is Sister Maria doing out here?'

'Talking to a supermodel and an old man,' I said.

'What?'

'That's who else is in the house.'

Then I told her both versions of the Stella Diaz story before her freckles all flew off in confusion. First I told her Chiquita's version – that Stella Diaz was secretly her mother. Then Sister Maria's version – that Chiquita was imagining things.

Bernadette went quiet for a moment. Stunned.

I thought it all through, as much as I could, and said,

'If Stella Diaz is here, maybe Chiquita's telling the truth.'

'You think Sister Maria's lying? Why? Why are they out here in the middle of nowhere?'

'I don't know,' I said. 'I've told you all I know.'

'Honestly?' Bernadette asked. 'I mean, how can I trust you that this is everything?'

I promised her on my grandad's life it was really everything. Not that 'everything' made any sense at the moment.

'Maybe they're looking for Chiquita,' Bernadette suggested.

'Chiquita only ran away an hour ago at the very most. How would her mother have got here so fast? She would be at least in London or, more likely, some foreign place,' I said, adding, 'That's if Stella Diaz is her mother.'

Bernadette held her head as if it was hurting with all the information. 'But why would Sister Maria lie to you?'

We didn't have time to think of an answer to this because we heard the cars starting.

We waited, hardly daring to breathe. Maybe they'd seen exactly where we'd run to and were coming to get us . . .

The cars drove past us and were gone.

'What shall we do now?' Bernadette asked.

It was getting really cold. I thought we should see if the house was left empty and we could find shelter in there.

'What if they come back?' Bernadette stopped holding her head and rubbed her ankle. 'They might kill us.'

'Are nuns allowed to kill people?'

'Well, they're not allowed to tell enormous lies so who knows what might happen.'

I said I didn't care what happened, I was so cold now that being killed seemed just an imaginary problem in comparison to freezing.

The lights weren't on anywhere in the house now so it looked as if it was safely empty but with the door, of course, locked. We walked around the house and found the back door was also locked but a tiny window above it was open a fraction. Bernadette stood on my shoulders and sort of slithered in, as if she was a natural-born burglar. Then she had a hard job pulling open some big old bolts on the back door but eventually we were in.

There was absolutely nothing in the house. Only some of the rooms had light bulbs that worked and there wasn't a stick of furniture.

In the kitchen there were only cupboards – no cooker, fridge, nothing. There were pipes and wires in the walls that showed where things might have been. I checked all the cupboards for food – nothing.

'It's not much warmer in here.' Bernadette shivered.

'At least it's dryer,' I said, shivering myself.

Then I noticed an electric heater on the wall and turned it on – it worked. I ran around and found one in every room. At least we wouldn't freeze as well as starve.

As we went into the bathroom upstairs we both realized that we were bursting to go to the toilet – lavatory. Sorry to mention that but it just helps show our adventure was a real one.

After we'd dealt with the highly realistic problem of being on a long adventure without a toilet break, we decided we should sleep in the little bedroom at the end of the upstairs landing. Being the smallest bedroom it would heat up quickest.

There were no blankets or beds, just bare wooden floors. We huddled round the heater, trying to make ourselves dry out and thaw out. I had no idea what to do next, except go to sleep, hungry, on the wooden floor.

Usually adventurers in a deserted house found tins of food or something. That always happened in books. Tins of beans at least, in the cupboard. Then someone would have a penknife to open them, which we didn't. I was getting so hungry I thought I'd scream.

Meanwhile, by the way, the nuns were going ape. All the girls had been given an early tea and sent to their rooms to read because Sister Patricia, in particular, was losing her mind. She now knew that three girls were missing. The hospital had phoned up about Bernadette again and the police had just gone off to search the moors with dogs. And Sister Maria also seemed to be missing, gone some-where in the best car with her mobile switched off.

Sister Patricia was just plucking up the courage to phone my mum to tell her I might be lost, when Sister Maria walked in saying she'd been for a long walk on the moors to meditate and pray and what on earth was going on? Sister

Patricia was very glad to see her because now Sister Maria could do the horrible job of phoning my mum. That kind of extremely important job was really for Sister Maria to deal with.

In case you're wondering how I knew this and I wasn't there, again I'm cheating and telling you what I found out later from Fiona and Sister Patricia. But I'm talking about a lot later, when a lot more very surprising things had happened.

Meanwhile in the deserted house I was thinking about a documentary I'd seen about starving people who'd boiled their own shoes to eat. I was going to ask Bernadette how she felt about this but she'd fallen asleep. Then I fell asleep too.

We were totally exhausted and we'd forgotten to lock the back door.

CHAPTER
TWENTY-FIVE

The room had become very overheated in the night. And very stuffy with Bernadette smell. But it was Bernadette who woke up complaining and clambering over me to get out of the little bedroom.

'I'm so hot, I'm suffocating.' She struggled to get the door open. 'I have to get out of here.'

Still half asleep, I was crawling around the floor, thinking of telling Bernadette to calm down, when Bernadette flung the door open and screamed. Then someone outside the door screamed.

Chiquita was standing there with a half-eaten bar of chocolate held up to her face.

At that moment we didn't care about anything – we just wanted that chocolate.

'We've been starving all night,' I said. 'It's brilliant you're here but we have to eat your chocolate.'

'I was asleep downstairs,' she said, handing the chocolate to me. 'I'd been wandering around the moors, lost for hours, and then I saw the house. The back door was open. I called out to see if anyone was here but you must have been already asleep. It was really dark night when I found this place. I was just so tired I went straight to sleep by the kitchen radiator.'

'Downstairs all night with chocolate?' Bernadette looked as if she'd lose her mind.

Chiquita divided up another bar she had in her pocket. We stuffed our faces and I quickly told her about Sister Maria and Stella Diaz being in this very house the night before.

Chiquita stared at me. 'Why would she be here?'

'I don't know. Sister Maria was shouting at her that she'd made a mistake, that she was wrong about something.'

'Tell her the other bit,' Bernadette said all crookedly, her mouth full of chocolate.

'Oh yes,' I said. 'Sister Maria told me—' Then I realized I had to be careful how I put this, so it wouldn't really upset Chiquita. 'I asked Sister Maria about Stella Diaz being your mother, back at school and it was a bit weird—'

'She said you made it up,' Bernadette interrupted.

Chiquita looked furious and her eyes sparked with tears. 'I didn't!' she shouted at Bernadette. 'I would recognize my own mother!'

'Of course you would.' I tried to calm her down. 'It's just Sister Maria – she says one thing and then she's out here in the middle of nowhere shouting at your mother.'

Chiquita wasn't interested in Sister Maria for now. She was only interested in her mother. 'Do you think she got my letter at the make-up company?'

'I don't know,' I said. 'I can't figure all this out at all.'

'Why would they be here and not at school?' Chiquita asked. 'Why ...?'

There were a thousand questions to ask but suddenly we heard dogs barking outside. The back door opened and in came a policeman who shouted: 'In here!'

And we were caught.

CHAPTER TWENTY-SIX

Bernadette was rushed away in one police car. The policeman in the passenger seat of our car told us all about the emergency of her operation and how my mum and grandad were being phoned this instant to say I was safe, because otherwise they were going to drop everything and rush to the school.

'What about Chiquita's mum?' I asked.

'I don't know anything about that,' he said. 'Probably worried sick like everyone else.'

'Is she at the school?' Chiquita asked, looking tearful.

'I don't know. This was a very silly thing to do, girls,' the policeman driving said. 'People die out on those moors at night.'

The passenger policeman looked at him and said, 'No need to scare them, Mike.'

'Well,' Mike said, 'they need to know what they did.'

The policemen didn't talk for a while. We drove down towards the school and I noticed Chiquita was really crying now. Just silently, tears pouring down her beautiful face.

'Maybe your mum will be at the school and everything will be wonderful from now on,' I said.

She looked at me and wiped her eyes. 'It's too weird,' she said. 'Why would she be in that place talking to Sister Maria? Why did Sister Maria tell you I was a liar? I wonder who the man was?'

'I don't know. He was old and rich-looking.'

Chiquita was quiet for a while, then said, 'It's so weird. I'd given up on her. I wasn't going to London this time. I just wanted to go away. Maybe live in a hotel by the seaside. I've run away like that before. Just to get away from school. It was stupid. I'd have run out of money eventually anyway. I don't get rich until I'm eighteen. I just have a pocket-money account now. I just had to get away.'

We were coming through the school gates.

'But why? I thought we were friends,' I said. 'I thought we had made a plan about you coming to my house in the holidays.'

'I know,' she said, and turned her head away from me. 'You are a very nice person.'

She didn't seem to want to talk any more. I tried to think of something to bring her back, something good.

'Maybe Stella Diaz has changed,' I said. 'Maybe now she's a nice person and will be a proper mum.'

'Don't,' Chiquita said. 'I don't want to think hopeful thoughts. Maybe she only showed up to tell Sister Maria I'm not her daughter, yet again. There's no point getting hopeful.'

She cried quietly for the rest of the journey. I couldn't think of anything else to say that didn't sound as if I was being hopeful.

I wondered about Bernadette's parents. Would they come from Hong Kong? Would they take her away after the operation so she could be happy?

In the school, the police took us straight to Sister Maria's office. She looked tired. She looked as if she'd been crying. She didn't look like normal Sister Maria at all.

The policemen told her where they'd found us and that Bernadette had been taken straight to hospital.

'Good, good,' Sister Maria said, seeming as if she wasn't really listening. 'The old farmhouse? They were in the old farmhouse?'

Then she frowned at us. She must have realized that the kids running around had been us and we'd probably seen Stella Diaz.

The policeman said they had to be getting on and they'd call back later to finish their report.

We were alone with Sister Maria. She didn't start the frightening staring that I'd expected. She reached inside her desk drawer and took out a clean white handkerchief. She blew her nose, very delicately, but it was still surprising that she would do something so ordinary.

She tucked the handkerchief into her sleeve and said in a tired, sad voice: 'Katherine. You go to your room, get washed and change your clothes, then go to the dining room where some breakfast has been put out for you. The other girls are in the chapel for Sunday Mass. When they come out for recreation you're not to join them. You're to stay in the dining room. You are in the most serious trouble it's possible for a pupil to be in at this school. I will have to decide—'

Chiquita impatiently interrupted whatever Sister Maria was going to say next. 'Why was my mother in the old farmhouse?'

'Wait, Chiquita, I will explain everything to you privately. Off you go, Katherine,' Sister Maria said.

I smiled at Chiquita as I went out. Perhaps she was going to get good news about her mother. Chiquita's big brown eyes seemed to be telling me she didn't want me to leave. Didn't want to hear whatever the truth was all on her own. But she was going to have to.

I washed my face and brushed my teeth. I wasn't sure what to put on. I was in the most serious trouble. Expelled? If I was going to be expelled maybe I shouldn't put on my school uniform. I started to feel very depressed when I looked at the uniform. The thoughts about Mum's money came in my head again. Poor Mum, all that money she'd spent on my things for school. And now I might be kicked out.

Still, seeing as the uniform was paid for I might as well wear it one last time. Maybe we could alter it when I got home so I could use it as normal clothes in some way. Being sent home would have the advantage that I could talk to Grandad. I'd tell him everything and he'd help me see how

I could avoid making such a mess of everything in future.

I didn't feel like Katie Milk, the girl I'd been in London, imagining that if she went to a boarding school she'd be just great and solving crimes and so on. I felt like useless Katherine Milne in a real boarding school, who'd nearly made Bernadette miss her operation out of stupidity, who couldn't be in boarding school a week without making herself an unpopular weirdo. Even Chiquita, who had no one in the world except nuns, would rather run away to some hotel and be alone for ever than be friends with me. And the more I thought about the stupid things I did, the more I didn't blame anyone for not liking me.

CHAPTER
TWENTY-SEVEN

There was juice and bread and butter set out for me in the dining room. I ate every crumb, drank all the juice and then I had the realistic feeling of wanting to go to the toilet – lavatory.

I waited a while, trying to be obedient to the staying-in-the-dining-room orders, but then I had to go. I thought if I went out the side door by the kitchen I'd stand less chance of being spotted by Sister Maria than in the main corridor.

Out by the kitchen, I realized I'd made a mistake and had no idea where the toilets would be in this nuns' part of the building. And it would probably be worse to be caught in the nuns' toilet than be caught in the main corridor anyway.

I was about to retrace my steps when I heard a banging sound from inside a cupboard just by the back door. Then I heard Chiquita's voice shouting for help.

I tried the cupboard door: it was locked.

'Chiquita, it's me, Katie!'

'Get me out, Katie! Get me out, quick. Sister Maria is trying to kidnap me!'

Kidnap? This was too exciting to be true. But I couldn't think how to open the door.

There was an axe lying on a pile of wood outside the back door. Could I axe the cupboard door open without killing Chiquita or chopping my own arms off?

Luckily I didn't have to find this out because suddenly there was a crash and the little door Chiquita was trapped behind burst open.

Chiquita fell out, panting. 'I saw it was an old lock,' she said. 'I thought if I kept kicking it would break.'

I was very impressed with this new door-kicking Chiquita. Even if, now I looked at it, it was a very old flimsy lock.

'Kidnapped?' I asked her, just in case she'd actually said something less interesting and I was getting carried away.

'Sister Maria is a maniac. She pushed me in that storeroom and locked it,' Chiquita said. 'We have to get away from here.'

Chiquita hurried me out of the back door and into the bushes. These were dense old bushes that had a sort of natural tunnel inside. We crawled through until we were far away from the back door, and down the side of the school.

'This is a good hiding place,' Chiquita panted. 'We have to hide, Katie. Sister Maria's totally crazy.' She caught her breath and then said that Sister Maria had gone berserk in the office. Telling her off for writing to Stella Diaz, calling her ungrateful and stupid. 'Then she told me she was going to take me away to where Stella Diaz will never find me.'

'She doesn't want her to find you?'

'She kept saying Stella Diaz was no good and she wasn't going to let me fall into her clutches. She says she's the one who's been like a mother to me and she's keeping me. Then she dragged me out of the office and locked me in that little room. She's gone insane.'

It did seem pretty like the behaviour of someone insane. Still, I was glad for Chiquita that it wasn't all a lie about Stella Diaz.

I tried to think. It seemed we were well-hidden in the bushes, so unless Sister Maria called the police with dogs to come back, she wouldn't find us.

Would she get the police if she was a crazed kidnapper? But then, would the police believe two girls who'd just been arrested for running away – or would they believe a beautiful, seemingly kind nun? My head was bursting again.

'Why would Sister Maria be doing such things?'

'I don't know,' Chiquita said. 'She said she was going to get her belongings and then take me away from Stella's evil influence. She'll know I'm gone soon. We should get out of here.'

'What we need,' I said, 'is to talk to an adult who'll believe our story, someone like my grandad. But we need to get to a phone. This stupid school and its no-mobiles rule.'

'Really stupid,' Chiquita said. 'I bought one on the internet but Sister Vincent confiscated it last term.'

'We'll have to use one of the phone boxes in the school,'

I started to say, but realized we'd be as insane as Sister Maria to go back into the school.

'The next nearest phone box is in the village,' Chiquita said. 'We'll be seen.'

'Not if we wait till dark.'

'Till dark? Here in the bushes?'

'That's the best I can think of.'

Chiquita thought for a while. 'It's the best I can think of too,' she said eventually.

We waited about ten minutes before I said, 'Maybe we should think of something better.'

'In a minute,' Chiquita said. 'I feel safe in here.'

'It's a good hiding place,' I agreed. 'And better than Bernadette's den. When she gets better we can show her it as a den.'

I don't know why I was talking about anything as childish as dens when we had real kidnapping and mad nuns to deal with, but Chiquita was right. It felt safe. It felt best to stay where we were, keep calm and not do anything frightening like taking action.

Unfortunately I did have to take urgent going-to-the-toilet action. I crawled through the bushes and told Chiquita not to listen. When I crawled back, I thought the incident had made Chiquita start thinking about people she associated with wee, but it turned out she was thinking about really serious matters.

'Do you think Bernadette will be OK?' she asked me, when I sat back beside her.

'I hope so.'

'Will the operation stop her smelling?'

'I think so. Maybe then she won't be so mean.'

'She's not always mean,' Chiquita said, surprisingly. Then she said, 'No one here is really mean except me.'

'What about Danielle?' I asked her.

'Oh, yes,' she said. 'But she didn't steal the money from Bernadette's desk.'

'How do you know?'

'Because it was me.'

I didn't want to hear this. I didn't want it to be her. 'You didn't even know there *was* money,' I said.

'When Sister Vincent sent me back to class you were all at netball or something. So I was in the classroom alone. I was nosing around in people's desks when I found the money. I had an idea I would hide it in Danielle's desk to get her in trouble but then I heard someone outside. I put the jar in my blazer pocket. All the time the fuss was going on I had it in my pocket. Then I moved it to the garden, hidden in a hole in that tree where I sit. I was meaning to move it to Danielle's room, but then it didn't seem worth all the fuss that was going on. So I left it outside Sister Maria's door when no one was looking.'

'So you didn't exactly steal it.'

'I just wanted to get my own back on Danielle for everything.'

It seemed to me that the stolen money jar was nothing at

all compared to the kidnapping and horror we were involved in now.

'I'd just forget about it,' I said. 'There's more important things to worry about.'

'It seemed like a good idea at the time but it was just stupid. As stupid as something Danielle would do.'

'Forget about it,' I said again. 'We've got bigger problems now.'

'I know,' Chiquita said. 'But I don't steal, I really don't. I was just nosing in people's desks because... Well, sometimes people have letters from their parents in their desks. I like to read them. To see the kind of things parents say. I know that's a bit creepy...'

'Not really,' I said, because it was a sad thing, not a creepy thing.

'Anyway, then after she'd done that speech about still wanting to catch the thief, Danielle got me on my own and said she was sure it was me. I thought if she could convince everyone I was a thief when I was innocent over the bracelet, then it would be so easy this time when I was guilty. And I had you being so nice to me but Danielle would make sure you ended up hating me for being a thief. So I just decided to run away and live on my own because I was too horrible to have friends and even if I had any, Danielle would always ruin it.'

Yet again, I couldn't believe the evilness of Danielle. 'What is wrong with her?'

Chiquita started crying. 'She once said she hated

me because I was spoilt – do you think that's the reason?

'I don't think she has reasons. She's just bad. Forget about her, we have Sister Maria to worry about now.'

Chiquita nodded, sniffing back tears. 'I just wanted to tell you about the money and why I'd acted weird.'

I was glad she trusted me enough to tell me the jam-jar secret. It did show we were proper friends. Proper friends in the middle of a kidnapping, stuck in the bushes, too scared to leave.

Actually, since I'd been to the toilet I was feeling a bit braver. I was going to suggest that maybe it was worth trying to sneak away now, instead of spending hours crouched down and getting hungry. But any words I might have said would have been drowned out by the noise coming from up by the front of the school.

A woman screaming and a car horn blaring – blaring, blaring and blaring again.

Not thinking about the danger of being spotted or re-kidnapped, we scrambled out of the bushes and ran to see what the commotion was.

It was a commotion and carry-on beyond anything I could imagine and almost beyond an escape of leprous one-eyed squashed-faced nuns.

CHAPTER
TWENTY-EIGHT

Sister Maria was screaming and fighting a very tall elegant woman in high heels – Chiquita's mother, Stella Diaz. She was pulling her hair, yanking her jacket, kicking her and shrieking at her.

Stella Diaz was trying to push Sister Maria away and shrieking back at her.

The old man from last night was looking very scared, blaring the car horn and shouting: 'Help, someone! Help us!'

Sister Vincent charged up, rummaging in her pockets of useful things, and pulled out her netball whistle. She blew it hard then bellowed, 'No, no! This is outrageous! Monstrous! Stop this instantly, stop it this instant!'

But Sister Maria tripped Stella Diaz to the ground, jumped on her and started pulling her hair as if she was trying to yank it all out. Stella Diaz fought back – she pulled off Sister Maria's veil then tried to grab at her short hair. As Sister Vincent blew the whistle, Danielle and the girls ran up to see. The old man blared the car horn and then Sister Patricia ran out waving a big stick.

Chiquita was watching what was going on with her hands up to her face, horrified.

Sister Patricia waved her stick around, making frightened squeaking noises.

The horn-blaring old man kept blaring until Sister Vincent shouted, 'For pity's sake, man, stop doing that and give me a hand here!'

She started to pull Sister Maria off Stella Diaz. The old man stopped blaring but looked too scared to help with the pulling. Sister Maria was crazy-looking – I wouldn't have liked to try pulling her either – but finally Sister Patricia dropped her stick and pulled at an arm. Then Sister Vincent got hold of Sister Maria by both arms, so she struggled and shouted, 'Let me go!' but couldn't escape.

Stella Diaz, very shaken up, got to her feet and stepped back towards the safety of her car. Then she dusted herself off and looked around at the watching schoolgirls. She stopped when she saw Chiquita.

'Chiquita?' she said, eyes filling with tears.

Chiquita looked at her, not sure what to do. It didn't matter. Crying and laughing at the same time, Stella Diaz ran over and hugged her. She was so tall and elegant that she was almost bent double over Chiquita, stroking her hair and sobbing, 'My baby, my little baby.'

Such talk could have been slightly sick-making but somehow it just seemed great.

Now I was watching with my hands up to my face. Not

horrified, but ready to hide my face because I thought I was going to start crying in front of everyone just out of surprise and happiness. I watched them and it was like the sun was shining from them. Everything was going to be like Chiquita's dreams.

Someone pulled at my sleeve. Danielle.

'What is this, what's happening? Why is Stella Diaz here?'

'She's Chiquita's mum,' I said, so pleased I could tell her this and see her know-all face go into shock.

'Stella Diaz is Chiquita's mother?' she gasped. 'That's ridiculous!'

Now Stella Diaz was holding Chiquita at arm's length, looking at Chiquita as if she was the most precious thing in the world. 'My baby girl. They told me you were dead.'

Chiquita seemed very confused. She looked for me and held out her hand so I would come over and hold it. 'This is my friend Katie,' she said. 'My best friend.'

Stella Diaz smiled at me with her gorgeous face smudged with tears and a bruise from Sister Maria swelling under her eye.

'Well look at you,' she said gently. 'The colour of milk. Katie Milk. My baby's friend.'

And I liked her immediately because somehow she'd known my nickname just by looking at me.

Sister Maria was still struggling. She was trying to bite at Sister Vincent's hands and shouting to Stella Diaz: 'You're not a fit mother! Look at you. Lanky, common-as-muck gold-digger! She's insane, don't believe a word she says. Can't you tell she's mad? Just look at her!'

Chiquita's mother looked very nice actually, considering she was all bashed about. She had beautiful clothes and the shiniest hair I'd ever seen. Long, black and wavy to the waist like Chiquita's. And she wasn't the one acting like a maniac: she was calm, although very sad.

'She'll go to jail,' she told Chiquita quietly. 'That's my lawyer over there. He says that what she's done amounts to kidnapping.'

Kidnapping? How brilliant – suddenly here I was, Katie Milk again, right slap bang in the middle of the happy end to my friend's kidnapping.

'So you want to be my mother?' Chiquita asked.

Stella made a tired sigh as she spoke. 'Of course I do. You belong with me. Not her. Not with your father's awful, rotten sister.'

'It's you that's rotten!' Sister Maria screamed.

'Sister? She's my aunt?' Chiquita gasped.

'That's enough, Maria!' Sister Vincent bellowed, trying to get the writhing nun in her arms to hold still.

'Don't listen to her, Chiquita!' Sister Maria writhed and yelled. 'She's a liar! She's ruined everybody's lives. You belong to my family! She's a lying, thieving illegal immigrant!'

Stella Diaz looked at Sister Maria with pity. 'That's how they got rid of me before,' she said, in her slightly American, slightly Spanish accent. It was an accent that sounded as strange and beautiful as she was. 'Yes, she's your father's sister,' Stella told Chiquita. 'Your father was a good man. He'd come to Guatemala to work for charity. That's when he met me. Fell in love with me. We got married. But when we came to England, his family went on and on that I'd married him for money, that I'd married him to get to England. Not long after you were born he got very sick with cancer. It was harder for him to stand up to them. He stopped trusting me. He didn't really trust them either. He loved you, though, baby. That's why he left everything to you.'

She hugged Chiquita tight. I shifted from foot to foot with impatience, desperate for her to stop with the hugging and get on with the story. Finally she did, talking so quietly to Chiquita that I kept panicking I'd miss some juicy detail.

'When your father died, I had nothing. And they kept trying to make me leave their house and leave you with them. They offered me money to leave, they called me names all the time. You have to remember I was very young. Only just twenty-two. From a small village in Guatemala, where I had a poor family who I couldn't afford to go home to. I was thinking the worst; I was thinking I would have to steal from the awful Morris family to get you and me away to Guatemala. Then two men came to the door telling me they were from immigration. I had to go to their office and answer some questions or I was in danger of being locked up and then deported.

'I wanted to take you with me but they said it wouldn't

take long. I was confused and scared because I was a silly, half-educated girl. I had my meeting with the men and they said they'd have to look into my case further but I could go home. When I got home everyone was gone. Including you. My husband's parents and you were gone. I realized it must have been them that had got the immigration people to take me away and interview me. They were very rich, powerful people who everyone listened to. I didn't know what to do. I knew them, I knew they'd taken you somewhere to hide you.' She brushed her hair back from her face, trying not to cry.

Chiquita frowned, trying to take it all in. 'But I don't understand...'

'I don't because...' I said, even though it wasn't really my business.

Stella smiled at me, then at Chiquita. 'I know, babies, it's such a horrible story—'

'We can handle it,' I butted in again, terrified she might decide not to tell us all of it.

Stella made a sad little laugh. 'OK, Katie. It's me that can't handle remembering really. But ...' She took a breath then went on. 'Anyway, that night the police came to the house. There'd been a car crash. Everyone in the car was dead, burned up, unidentifiable. I asked them about you but the police said the people in the car had been driving very fast, gone off a motorway bridge. They'd gone into a lorry carrying pressurized oxygen to a hospital. There'd been a massive explosion, lots of people burned to ash. They'd only known who the car belonged to by looking at the number plates that had gone past the motorway speed cameras just before the accident. They said if the investigators could find anything for me, they'd be in touch.'

Suddenly she changed from being sad to being angry. 'I thought they'd killed you. I couldn't stand staying in their house a minute longer. I left for London with nothing, to start my life again. But you hadn't been in the car. They'd already left you here, with Sister Maria, who brought you up to think I'd abandoned you. Then I got your letter last week. I came here right away and Sister Maria said you weren't here. But I had your letter. I tried to talk sense to her last night. I didn't want a horrible scene with you involved so I agreed to go to some farmhouse belonging to the Morris family … The woman is crazy. But it's over now. All I want is to take you away from here, Chiquita, and make up for lost time.'

Chiquita was just staring at her, bewildered. So was Sister Patricia, who'd come to stand by us, listening to the horrible story.

'But Sister Maria showed me a letter from you, an official letter saying it was lies I was your daughter,' Chiquita said.

'Whatever she showed you must have been fake. Sister Maria has never been in touch with me.'

'Don't listen to her!' Sister Maria screamed and writhed.

Chiquita still didn't seem as if she could believe her

luck. 'She said she'd been trying to get you to come here for years.'

'That's lies,' Stella Diaz said. 'It's just lies. I thought you were dead.'

'Oh dear, oh dear,' said Sister Patricia.

'Don't listen to that woman! She's insane!' Sister Maria screamed, looking very insane.

The old lawyer man stepped up with some papers. 'I have been gathering information. I have here birth certificates, marriage certificates and you'll notice there is no death certificate for Chiquita. After weeks of investigation the crash investigators said there were no remains of a child in the car. This investigators' conclusion was given to Sister Maria, who told the police that Stella had returned to Guatemala. I presume they had no reason to doubt the word of a convent headmistress.'

Stella Diaz shook her head. 'I was a little idiot. Why didn't I think that they'd have brought you here? I knew Sister Maria – she'd visited the house several times. Why didn't I think of looking here?'

'Why didn't you?' I asked her.

She shook her head again and started crying. So easy to see she was Chiquita's mother now – they cried in exactly the same way, all gushing out, never mind who was looking. 'I wasn't thinking straight when they told me about the crash, I was just torn up with grief.' She looked at Chiquita, her enormous brown eyes full of all the sad thoughts in the world. 'I thought you were dead and I had to get away.

I went to London and lost myself in the crowd of office cleaners who work from dusk to dawn. I changed my name because I was still afraid the immigration people might get me. One day, the strange but kind woman I worked for explained to me that I was perfectly legal and could use my real name. Then she said, "I don't know why you're a cleaner. A beautiful girl like you, why don't you look up the name of some modelling agencies in the Yellow Pages and just turn up there?" I thought I was too old – models are usually younger than twenty-two – but I just had the look some designer wanted. So that was that, I said goodbye to my kind boss and her funny peach-coloured uniforms and became a model.'

What?

'Not peach,' I said hoarsely. 'Apricot.'

'Yes, Katie,' she said. 'Apricot. How did you know that?'

Before I could explain, Sister Maria managed to break free of Sister Vincent's strong grip and ran screaming down the drive. Sister Vincent started to run after her, blowing her whistle. Sister Maria stumbled and Sister Vincent jumped on her, veil nearly flying off because inconveniently this wasn't her elasticated action veil. But, despite that problem, she wrestled and Sister Maria was caught again.

She didn't fight any more. She kept her head down, crying bitterly as Sister Vincent brought her back.

'I should take her to the infirmary,' Sister Vincent said, looking very upset.

Then she looked apologetically at Stella Diaz. 'The rest of us didn't know. She told us the child was an orphan. We believed what she told us. I'm so sorry. You must do as you see fit, but it seems to me Sister Maria is a very sick woman. We have a quiet convent in Ireland, where nuns who've become ill are looked after. It's in the countryside. They grow vegetables and live quietly. If you'd let me send her there it would be very kind of you.'

Stella Diaz nodded. 'As long as I never have to see her again,' she said, wiping her eyes. She must have had some special expensive mascara because despite all the crying it was only smudged a bit. 'And as long as she never contacts my daughter again.'

Sister Maria sobbed more loudly, clinging onto Sister Vincent like a child. 'I look after Chiquita,' she whimpered. 'She's my brother's child, she should be with me.'

Sister Vincent led Sister Maria to the infirmary.

At first I was disappointed not to see Sister Maria hauled off to jail by the police – but then as I watched her go with Sister Vincent, all broken and pathetic, I remembered how she'd been when I first met her. Like a beautiful, cool stone angel. It seemed very sad to see her all collapsed and broken like this.

Unbelievably, just as I was about to try again to tell Stella Diaz about Auntie Apricot being my auntie, Danielle stepped up with her hand held out to shake, and her best smile on her face.

'Now there's a bit of peace and quiet, I thought I'd

introduce myself and say if there's anything me or any of Chiquita's friends can do to help . . .'

Stella Diaz shook her hand but looked at Chiquita. 'Who's this?' she asked.

Chiquita looked at Danielle. 'I think she's one of those people like Sister Maria, who seems very nice but is really a liar and an awful person.'

Stella dropped Danielle's hand and said sharply, 'Well, you better get lost then, hadn't you, blondie.'

And Danielle looked like she'd been smacked in the face with a wet deer head.

CHAPTER
TWENTY-NINE

About a week later Sister Vincent drove me to visit Bernadette in hospital.

Sister Vincent was temporarily in charge of the school. Sister Maria had been sent to the very quiet convent in Ireland to get help from people who knew about dealing with nuns who'd gone crazy. I had so much to tell Bernadette, I couldn't wait.

In hospital, there was a great sight: Bernadette grinning like I'd never seen her grin before. Both her parents were by her bed and she was sitting up, surrounded by teddy bears, magazines and flowers, wearing a very orange nightie that was a bit of a mistake with ginger hair.

'Guess what,' she said, grinning even more. 'My dad is going to try and get a job in London next year so we can all live together all the time.'

Her mum, also very ginger-haired, smiled at her dad, the most ginger of all.

'Well,' her mum said to Sister Vincent, 'there's more to life than money.'

Sister Vincent smiled and nodded.

Bernadette's dad nodded too and looked sad, as if he'd only just realized this fact about money.

'This is all brilliant, Bernadette,' I said. 'But guess what...' And I quickly told her the whole story about Sister Maria being nuts and secretly Chiquita's auntie and Chiquita being rescued by her mother. Right up to the most brilliant moment where Danielle was completely humiliated in front of the whole school by a top supermodel.

Bernadette's parents stared at me, then they stared at Sister Vincent.

'Is all this true?' they asked her.

'I'm afraid so. Most unfortunate.'

'Also brilliant,' Bernadette said. 'A mad nun, not in the attic but actually wandering around in charge of us. How brilliant.'

'I'm not sure I'd say it was brilliant.' Sister Vincent shook her head. 'But at least it's turned out for the best.'

It *had* turned out for the best. And tons of other things had happened.

My mum had been up to the school in her little bashed car and told Sister Vincent that she was horrified by what had been going on, and she didn't want me in a school where nuns were mad and children were kidnapped. Sister Vincent had apologized to her and promised her the school would be far more normal now. My mum only allowed me to stay at the school because I begged her but I had to promise not to run away again or else...

As Bernadette predicted, Fiona and Sarah seemed like best friends now, going around being nice but uninteresting together. It seemed to make them a lot happier than being dragged into adventures with un-nice but very interesting people – mentioning no names beginning with 'B'.

Chiquita would soon be back from London, where she'd been allowed to stay two weeks with her mother, so she could get to know her properly. And, as a special rule for this term, Stella was allowed to come and take Chiquita out every weekend.

Stella Diaz was going to put a manager in her New York business and move the headquarters to London. Possibly next term Chiquita would leave completely, live with Stella Diaz and go to a nice school in London. For the time being Chiquita said she'd prefer to stay in the same school as me and Bernadette, her old and new best friends.

Stella Diaz had also scared the wits out of Grandad, or so he said, by turning up on his doorstep in a big limousine and going on about how she wanted to meet him because Auntie Apricot had been so kind to her when she was just a cleaner. And now I'd been kind to Chiquita, so she felt our family must be amazing and she wanted to meet all of us and how wonderful that fate had brought us all together ... Grandad said he'd made her a cup of tea and all the neighbours were hanging out of their windows watching her when she'd left. They were possibly a bit 'underprivileged' and not used to famous models in their street, so they were staring and shouting, 'Hey, Stella!'

Just to be friendly and to cover the embarrassment of the neighbours, Grandad said, 'Well, best of luck then, and if you need a good security guard for your headquarters in London, give me a try.'

Next thing he knew, she said she was looking for a nice, trustworthy bodyguard who was interesting to talk to and didn't look like a gorilla. Apparently most bodyguards looked like gorillas and were generally not interesting to talk to. But, being famous, she did need a bodyguard to go places, so all Grandad's security-guard training would be fine. He could get some younger assistants for any fast running that was needed, but he would be the one she relied on to keep her safe, organize the young ones and have interesting conversations with her about Auntie Apricot, who she seemed to be slightly obsessed with, and didn't see the annoying side of her at all.

So off Grandad went. He left the job at Boots, left other people to guard the toothpaste, and started a whole new glamorous life. He'd no more time to just watch television and be lonely; he was out seeing the world and having real adventures.

Just a week after he'd gone, Mum sent me a magazine with a picture of Stella at a film opening – and beside her was Grandad in a black suit, talking into a head mike, looking like a very serious bodyguard. Obviously I'd put the picture up in my locker so people like Danielle could see it. She did and just stuck out her tongue at me, which was pretty pathetic and childish. But what could she say?

Practically the whole school had heard Stella Diaz tell her to get lost.

Danielle was losing her popularity by the minute. I noticed Indira the princess was frantically trying to make friends with me these days. Well, I'd have to see. I had quite a lot of friends already.

I hoped Sister Vincent wasn't quite right in saying that the school was going to be very normal from now on. What fun would that be? After all, although boarding-school life hadn't been quite as full of crimes as the books I'd read, it had been quite interesting so far.

I needn't have worried. Bernadette didn't smell of wee any more but she still had very good ideas.

'You know what, Katie?' she said one night after she came back from hospital. 'If Sister Maria was wandering around secretly mad, perhaps there are other secretly mad nuns to catch.'

'There could be,' I said, pleased about the idea. And you'll notice that she'd finally, finally given in and started calling me Katie.

'Maybe,' she said, going into her scary-story voice, 'maybe, after she's turned our lights out at night, Sister Ita becomes monstrous and crawls around the attic, making noises to try and scare us out of our wits because she secretly hates us. So at night she tries to send us nuts. I bet if we listen carefully we can hear her, crawling around and making horrific noises.'

'Shnurguh, shnurguh?'

'Exactly!' Bernadette screamed with laughter so loud that Sister Ita herself burst into our room and turned the light on. Her face was redder than red and I wondered if that came from getting out of breath crawling around the attic and making noises.

'That's enough now. No more talking or silly behaviour,' she said. 'You two need to behave yourselves the rest of this term and there's to be no more nonsense.'

But obviously there would be a lot of nonsense. And kidnappings and adventures and crimes and so on.

In the first book about the bizarre but loveable
Strega-Borgia family, it's all go at StregaSchloss.
There are beasts in the basement, rats in the modem
and an elderly relative in the freezer . . .

'Original, challenging, entertaining and, frankly,
bizarre . . . warm and hilarious, highly individual
style which crackles with energy' *Guardian*

'It's a gallimaufry of ghastly giggly stuff . . . good,
disgusting fun' *Financial Times*

'A magical romp in the witty British tradition'
The Times

'Debi Gliori . . . reveals a talent for wild comedy,
linguistic invention and pastiche . . . Wonderful stuff'
Daily Telegraph

'A rollicking good tale . . . a book that radiates
enjoyment' *Independent*

CORGI BOOKS
0 552 54757 3

PURE DEAD WICKED

Disaster strikes at StregaSchloss in the fabulous
second book in the PURE DEAD... saga.

The roof of the ancestral pile is beyond
repair and the Strega-Borgia family have to move
out while the builders move in. Pandora, Titus,
Damp and all (including the beasts) decamp to
the local hotel. But the talking tarantula, the
frozen granny and a mysterious trickle of
tincture are left behind. Is that a good idea?

'A relentless narrative pace. There's only one
tempo permitted – fast-forward ... wonderful
read-aloud material' *The Times Educational Supplement*

'Barbed, sidesplitting farce ... pedal-to-the-metal
page turner' *Kirkus Reviews*

'A breezy combination of wild caricature,
computer-savvy contemporary sensibility
and lavatorial jokes' *Sunday Times*

CORGI BOOKS
0 552 54847 2